80AD
The
Sudarshana

(Book 4)

Aiki Flinthart

ISBN-13: 978-0-9945660-6-5
Computing Advantages & Training P/L

Discover other titles by Aiki Flinthart at:
http://aikiflinthart.weebly.com/

Cover Art by : Jason Seabaugh

Review:
"This story is very unique. The premise is immensely entertaining. It's a great story!".......Chilli Tween Reads October 31st 2011

NOTE: this series is written with the young adult agegroup in mind. Having said that, thousands of adults have read and enjoyed them as well. Please bear this in mind when reading and leaving feedback.

80AD

Level Four

The Sudarshana.

FENG ZHUDAI

Feng Zhudai paced the length of his room, his lean body stiff with barely-controlled anger as he stalked back and forth. The aura of his fury filled the small, stark space. The servant who had sought him out knelt on the floor and dared to clear his throat to remind the sorcerer of his presence. Zhudai stopped, sliding slender hands into the long sleeves of his black silk robe. Staring out a window, he ignored the exquisitely trimmed and tamed garden outside.

Surrounded by the opulence and extravagance of the Emperor's Palace in Xijing, Zhudai chose to decorate his suite with nothing more than a large calligraphy painted on red silk, a low, black table and a sleeping mat. The walls were bare and the floors just well-scrubbed wood. He did it deliberately, knowing that his severity made the fat, overindulged servants of Emperor Han Zhangdi uncomfortable. They were frightened of him. Even the military men, lead by General Ban Chao, hesitated to come into the presence of the Emperor's Advisor.

He spun to face his cowering manservant, scowling. "And you say that after he arrived from Luoyang, the Emperor met with Ban Chao for two hours this morning?"

The servant nodded, bowing until his nose touched the floor.

Zhudai paced again. "That man is getting above himself," he muttered. "It might be time for a change of scenery for the General." Annoyed he had spoken unwisely in front of a servant, he waved an impatient hand at the cringing man. "I want you to track the General at all times. I want to know everything he says and does. You will be rewarded handsomely. Present yourself to my secretary at once and tell him so. Do you understand?"

Visibly relieved, the servant nodded and bowed himself out backwards.

Zhudai frowned again, tapping long-nailed fingers on the sleeve of his robe. Perhaps it was time to have another chat with Baiyu. His childhood friend had once been close to the General and had been a Royal Tutor to the young Emperor. Perhaps he could be persuaded to give some insight into what Ban Chao was planning with the Emperor.

He had been away too long. Trying to prevent the otherworld travellers from reaching this land had delayed his plans. His absence from the Emperor's capital in Luoyang gave Ban Chao a chance to worm his way into the Emperor's affections. Zhang was only twenty-four years old: a mere boy besotted with his Consort, the new Empress Dou; still mourning the death of his mother, the Empress Dowager Ma; and not wise enough to choose his advisors carefully. He needed to be reminded to whose words he should be listening. General Ban Chao, and possibly the young Empress, might just have to be removed before the *ri shi.*

Smiling, Zhudai let the thought of that day calm him. Yes. On the day of the *ri shi*, all would be finished. The outworlders lured here by Baiyu's pathetic attempt at magic would be too late and too weak to rescue Baiyu. By now they were stuck somewhere in India – where he had personally supervised the beginnings of a war between two kingdoms in their path. His agents were well paid to ensure the four interlopers would never make it through another portal. So, with Baiyu safely locked away and the General and Empress removed, there would be no-one to oppose Zhudai's ascendancy into immortality…

CHAPTER ONE

Jade Lockyer stepped into a grey-lit world of thunderous noise. It wasn't just noise. It was a shocking, almost solid, booming that deafened and pounded the breath from her body. She flinched away. Her mare took instant exception and reared up with a whinny that was lost in the din. Only luck made Jade clench her hand in time to keep hold of the reins. The horse backed up and danced to one side, tossing her head. Her hooves slipped on the glistening black rock underfoot and she almost fell. Pulling the mare's head down, Jade laid a hand on the long nose and gripped tightly. She yelled a *command* word into the animal's ear and watched for a second to make sure she settled.

Jade took stock of her surroundings. Ahead, pale light filtered through a vast wall of water plunging past a huge opening. She seemed to be in a large, stone cavern, behind a waterfall. Her hair lifted as the white torrent pushed a damp breeze into the cave. Droplets of moisture clung to everything, making the floor slippery and the walls drip. Every breath she drew of the laden air smelled of moss and fresh water.

As soon as it was clear there was no real danger, she turned to help the others coming through the Portal behind her.

Phoenix strode through, looking every inch the barbarian warrior with wild black hair, a coarse brown shirt and iron-studded leather arm and leg guards. In one hand he held his mount's reins, in the other he clutched Blódbál, the enchanted sword given to him by Thor. Five of the seven blood-rubies embedded in the handle of his Life-dagger, sparkled at his hip as he stepped past Jade. Smears of dried blood darkened his clothes and skin. He looked exhausted but determined - a far cry from the cocksure, careless thirteen year old boy who had awoken just two weeks ago to find himself trapped in an unfamiliar body in an unreal world.

After him came Brynn, yanking on the reins of his frightened pony. The young Breton boy had never ridden before their time in Svealand and the pony knew exactly who was boss. Looking a bit like an undersized Jedi in his stolen monk's robe, Brynn flinched at the onslaught of sound, shook his tousled auburn head and blinked in surprise. Recovering, he sent Jade a rueful, gap-toothed grin, pointed at his stubborn beast and shrugged.

The pony dug its front feet into the rock as it strained backward, brown eyes wild with fear. Only halfway through the glimmering portal, its rump would still be sticking out, into the Alexandrian dawn in faraway Egypt. Jade hurried forward. She *commanded* both his pony and Phoenix's grey stallion so they could be led aside to let Marcus through.

The handsome Roman emerged. If the roar affected him, the only sign he showed was a slight clenching of his jaw. His dark hair was trimmed much shorter than Phoenix's shoulder-length mop and his bare, soot-smudged arms were more tanned. His once-white Roman tunic was somewhat the worse for wear after their long night fighting in the Temple of Set. Dried blood crusted a shallow cut across his chest. Although obviously weary, he walked lightly and carried himself with his usual quiet dignity. He had fisted two sets of reins in one hand and held his long-bladed Svear sword in the other. A bow and quiver of arrows were slung across one shoulder and a short dagger sheathed at one hip.

Before long, all five horses stood quite calmly, as though they couldn't even hear the tumultuous booming that shook the chamber. In the few minutes it took for their eyes to adjust to the light, Jade noticed her friends all looked as tired as she felt. Maybe they should have stayed one more night in Alexandria. No, she dismissed the thought with regret, they had only five days to finish this Quest. They couldn't afford to waste any time.

She and Phoenix had already been trapped as Players in this two thousand year old game-world for two weeks too long. There was no telling how much time had passed in the real world. Any day now, the real-world game would be opened to the public domain on the internet and they might be swamped with other Players. Would there be any way of telling when the game was opened to the rest of the world? Some sort of sign in the heavens? An awareness that they weren't alone any more in a demo version? Or was this world actually real, as they'd been told back on level One in Albion? Jade glanced around the damp cave. It certainly felt real enough. In fact, she'd long since stopped even doubting it.

She sighed. At the beginning of this adventure she'd been quite hopeful that they'd be home in a few days. It had now been two weeks and things were tougher with each Level. It never seemed this hard in the books she read. They still had to finish Level Four and Five in order to get home and they were all exhausted.

Jade pressed her lips together and adjusted the hood of her cloak. Out of habit, she touched the half-amulet that hung about her neck. It was safe. The two halves had drawn her and Phoenix into this realm and she was fairly sure they'd need them to get home again – assuming they ever managed to get to Level Five and defeat Zhudai. If they didn't, she and Phoenix could face a lifetime, trapped in this other-world of ancient violence.

She shuddered and screwed up her nose in an effort to prevent the sting of tears. She'd started this game as an escape from her ordinary life; a way of diving into the sort of adventures she'd read about for years; a way of being something she was not. *Actually* being transported into the computer game had *so* not been part of her plan. Now she was stuck in a fantasy-world-real-world version of 80AD, somewhere deep in India, with a Quest to complete that she had no idea how to even begin.

Maybe she was just tired. She'd used a lot of energy up during the battle to save Brynn and release the Goddess Anuket in Egypt. With little sleep over the last forty-eight hours and days spent away from the forests her Elven heritage craved, she was worn out. Unfortunately, knowing why she felt miserable didn't mean she could help feeling that way.

Ignoring Marcus' disapproving gaze, she pulled out her herb bag. St John's Wort for depression and some barley grass for energy. That should do the trick. Marcus might think she could handle anything without the help of her herbs but she knew better. Her half-Elven avatar *needed* the herbs to supplement her magic. Without them, she just wasn't good enough to cope with this world.

Jade put the bag away and readjusted the weight of her backpack. Inside was the Hyllion Bagia – the bottomless bag that now held the *Sudarshana;* a silver, disc-shaped chakra weapon. Anuket had told them to return it to its rightful owner on the last night of the dying moon, so that's what they had to do.

Regrettably, Anuket had been big on cryptic predictions but a bit short on details – like *who* the rightful owner was; what broken thing would it fix; what person who had done wrong would be redeemed; and whose Empire it would unite. There was no way of knowing. All Jade knew, from previous game instructions, was that the

Quest had to be completed in the city of Punya-Vishaya, in India. Even that didn't help much. Wandering about a foreign city asking for the owner of a slab of pure silver was about as smart as wearing a sign on your forehead saying "please mug me".

No, they would have to find a more subtle way of tracing who it belonged to. Actually, first they'd have to find the city of Punya. OK, no: *first* they had to find a way out of this cave – if a way out even existed …

She shivered at that thought and hurried to join her friends. The shimmering Portal vanished. It was now simply three stones in the shape of a rough doorway, standing up against the cave wall.

Jade whispered a dozen little green lights into existence and floated them over her head. Using basic hand signals, the companions split up and began to search for an exit. With this illumination, it took only moments to discover that, short of going blindly through the waterfall, there appeared to be no other way out.

She, Marcus and Phoenix gathered at the white wall of water and stood, staring into it in forced silence. Phoenix tapped her on the shoulder. He pointed at the waterfall and shrugged. Next he pantomimed running and jumping, screaming, falling and dying. Then he twirled one finger in a circle around his temple. She nodded. Through a few gaps around the edge of the flow of water, she saw a river valley, far below. Too far. There was no way they or their horses would survive an excitingly-heroic jump through the cascade.

Jade scowled, pondering on the sort of sadists that must have programmed this game. Who on earth made the entrance to the fourth level of this digital world appear inside a dark, wet, exit-less cave? This was even worse than emerging into the airless offering chapel of Snefru's Shining Pyramid in Egypt last time. At least then they'd had Thor's hammer to help them get out of the building.

Even if they still had it, the Hammer wouldn't get them out of here.

Brynn had vanished somewhere into the darkness with his usual independence. Jade peered into the gloom, wondering where the orphaned ten year old had got to. He was better at getting himself into trouble than he was at getting out of it.

As though her thoughts had conjured him, Brynn appeared at her side. He waved a hand at her. His thin face split into a wide grin and his dark eyes sparkled with excitement. Jade sighed. He'd either found a way out or he'd found some treasure to steal. She followed his wiry figure into the depths of the cave, treading carefully on the slippery, broken floor.

There it was. Right at the very back of the cave: a tunnel. Mostly hidden by a rockfall that would have to be moved before the horses could get past, it certainly looked like the best chance to escape they'd found so far. To make sure, though, someone would have to follow it. There was no point in leading the horses into dead end.

Brynn tugged on her arm and pointed to himself then to the narrow gap at the top of the rockslide. Jade sent him a dubious look, shrugged and sent four little lights to bob around his head. Their glow cast a weird, greenish light on his eager young face.

The boy grinned and pulled a new leather sling out from under the oversized monk's robe he still wore. He didn't seem to regret the loss of his sword in Egypt but since he was better with a rock-sling than a blade, that wasn't surprising. She knew he must be more upset at losing his sophisticated set of lock-picks and reminded herself to get them replaced at the first opportunity. Having someone in their team who could pick locks was handy – especially considering the number of times they seemed to end up imprisoned in this insane time-space.

With a jaunty salute, Brynn clambered up the rockpile

and slipped through the opening. The glow of his witchlights faded and Jade was left to wait and exchange worried looks with Marcus, when he joined her.

A little way away, Phoenix slumped against a curving rock wall. Jade glanced over and saw him push off the rock, wiping irritably at the cold water that must have dribbled down his neck. He grimaced and looked around, probably for a dry place to sit. There wasn't one, so he slouched over to where she and Marcus waited.

She smiled wryly at him. From her point of view at least, this place was better than the endless, sand-storm ridden desert they'd been thrown into in Egypt; or the icy northern forest of Sweden. At least here she sensed the presence of forests not far away. Briefly, she longed for the cool green hills of England – modern or ancient – before dismissing the thought as pointless. They were in India – hopefully.

They had to focus on the here-and-now, not the past or the future. Getting herself and her friends through this game level was all that mattered. At least Phoenix was taking it more seriously now. He had begun this as though it was the sort of fun adventure every gamer dreamed of. Losing lives had changed him. As had Blódbál.

Jade looked down at the magic blade. Even now Phoenix's hand was wrapped around its hilt as though it was part of his body. He caught her look and glared back, his fingers tightening as if afraid she would try to take it off him. She turned away, uneasy. Although Thor had promised Phoenix would be able to control the sword's bloodlust, she doubted it would be simple. His impulsiveness and distrust of others was magnified by the sword's thirst for battle. He didn't think straight when he was under its power. She wished they could throw it away but they needed all the magical help they could get in this world. She would just have to keep a close eye on him and try to help him control his temper.

A quick look over at the tunnel entrance showed Brynn returning from his scouting mission and waving eager handsigns at them. She gathered he had found the path to be wide enough for the horses. So now all they had to do was move the rockslide that blocked it.

It took the better part of an hour to move enough small boulders to let the horses edge by. More than once, Jade wished they hadn't returned Thor's hammer. It had been so useful for breaking things. Now, they were forced to use pure physical labour. Phoenix, whose avatar's strength was impressive, looked exhausted. Brynn's face was pinched and even Marcus appeared close to the end of his endurance.

As she almost dropped yet another basalt block on her toe, Jade realised it wasn't just physical effort making them weary. A lack of sleep and food contributed. They had spent most of the last twenty-four hours sneaking through the streets of Alexandria, fighting the priests of Set and generally causing havoc and destruction.

Things were getting ridiculous – or ridiculouser, if there was such a word. They couldn't keep going like this or they would be too worn out to deal with whatever badguys the game threw at them. The minute they got down to open, dry land, they had to rest. She had no idea what time of day it was but it felt like a great time to sleep.

Finally, the task complete, they lead the horses up to the half-exposed entrance. Brynn tugged on Jade's arm, pointing up. Following his finger, she shivered. Above the curved tunnel opening a hideously life-like carving was etched deep into the black basalt rock: a snake. A rearing cobra, its hood spread wide; fangs bared. It seemed so real in the shifting half-light that she almost expected it to strike down at them.

What did it mean? Was it a warning or just some sort of street-sign saying "Snake Alley"? Maybe people lived in these caves and this was their way of naming the tunnels.

It was possible.

She glanced at the others and they exchanged rueful shrugs. It wasn't like they had a choice. They either went down this tunnel or they sat here forever. At a nod from Phoenix, Jade sent five of her little witchlights floating ahead, down the tunnel.

They revealed a man-made structure slicing deep into the mountain. Chisel marks were clearly visible in the black walls. Here and there were crude carvings of snakes – poor copies of the masterpiece above the entrance; perhaps done by workers laboriously hacking out the passage. Water dripped from cracks in the roof, staining parts of the stone an ominous, rust-red. It looked as though the walls bled. Jade shivered.

As though catching her feeling of apprehension, the horses balked at the opening. She was obliged to *command* them again before they would walk into the darkness. Leading, Phoenix drew Blódbál and nodded to Marcus. As the group stepped into the passageway, Jade paused. Her vague anxiety deepened to a cold, heavy sense of foreboding; a feeling that some ancient, malevolent power had somehow awakened, disturbed by their presence.

Her warning cry was lost in the roar of the waterfall. Before she could do anything, the horses panicked, rearing and striking out with sharp hooves. Around them, the earth trembled. Behind them, a new rockfall tumbled down in a cloud of dust, obliterating the tunnel entrance under tonnes of stone.

CHAPTER TWO

"No!"

It was the first clear word any of them had heard for awhile and the four looked at each other in surprise as Jade's cry rang out in the sudden silence following the earthquake's end. The waterfall's roar was muted to a dull rumble by the mass of rock blocking the tunnel.

Phoenix coughed, raked a hand through his unruly, dark hair and eyed the tumbled pile of stones with regret and resignation. Several enormous chunks had fallen, making clearing the opening again impossible.

"It's not like it makes much difference, really. We'd already decided to go this way, hadn't we?" He spoke the first few words in a normal voice and then dropped instinctively to a whisper as the sounds echoed back at him.

The others glanced around, nodded and heaved a collective sigh.

"I just don't like the idea that we're stuck in here." Jade voiced what they were all thinking.

For awhile, they stood, staring at the jumbled black rocks in silence. Then Brynn looked up at Phoenix, grinned and punched him lightly in the arm.

"I don't think this counts – it's an accident. Remember, too, that I got shoved into the cells of Set's temple, so you and I are even now: five-five."

Phoenix laughed, explaining to the others. "Brynn and I were comparing how many times we'd been stuck in prisons so far. We're up to five each, apparently. You two are on…um… three each, I think." He grinned at Jade who frowned up at him in bewilderment.

"Uh-huh." She blinked and shook her head. "I'm sure the importance of that will hit me soon and I'll be amazed. In the mean time, can we get on with it? Just before the earthquake, I was going to tell you that there's something down this tunnel. Something awful. I can feel it." She glanced into the darkness.

He sobered. He knew better than to ignore her 'feelings'. In this world, Jade was a half-Elf; attuned to all things magical and natural. Her senses had warned them several times so far and he'd be stupid to dismiss them.

"Right, let's stay on our toes then." He faced the shadows and gripped Blódbál trying to ignore its insidious message.

As always, the magic sword urged him to use it; to spill blood; to give in to its lust for battle. He was almost accustomed to it now but if he wasn't careful he'd get overconfident. If he did that, it would take over his body and turn him into a killing machine unable to distinguish friend from foe. He grimaced, remembering how near he'd come to murdering Marcus. A wry smile twisted his mouth. Actually, Marcus had been well able to defend himself, even against Blódbál's enchanted expertise. Still, he had to be on his guard. Next time he might pick on Brynn or Jade and their weapons skills weren't nearly as good as Marcus'.

They paused for a moment as Jade insisted Brynn exchange his cumbersome monk's robe for normal clothes and they all eat something. Whether it was from tiredness or uneasiness, Phoenix wasn't sure but nobody protested the delay or her mothering. They ate quickly and sparingly from the supplies given to them by Heron's housekeeper in Alexandria. Afterward, a little refreshed, they once more turned toward the blackness.

"We need a torch." Marcus peered along the dark tunnel.

"But we have Jade's lights," Brynn returned, defensive of her Spellweaver abilities.

The Roman raised an eyebrow at the youngster. "A flame will tell us which direction air is flowing through the caves. We can follow it to the outside."

"Oh." Brynn pulled down the corners of his mouth, considering. "Makes sense, I guess. I put some torches into the Hyllion Bagia back at Heron's place."

"Brynn!" Jade sounded scandalised. "Heron helped us. What else did you put in?"

The boy shrugged. "Nothing he'll miss much: a few extra skins of wine; a couple of pillows; a spare toga or two for Marcus; a cloak for me; a nice little crystal prism; a hammer; a…"

"Enough!" Phoenix interrupted. "I can't believe you did that. How could you steal from him?"

"Hey!" Brynn managed to look both offended and amused at the same time. "I *traded* stuff with him. I don't steal from friends. I gave him some of my Egyptian treasure but it was probably wasted on him – he just wanted to study it, not spend it."

Phoenix exchanged uncomfortable looks with Jade. They'd both assumed their little thief had stolen the goods. Face flaming, Jade apologised and pulled out the Bag. Sure enough, when Phoenix thrust his hand into its black maw and muttered 'torch', a long wooden shaft slapped into his palm.

Within a few moments, they had a smoky flame going and moved down the tunnel. Phoenix led, holding the torch out at chest height, trying to gauge air movement by its flickering. There was a faint but steady stream flowing toward them.

The tunnel went straight and slightly down for awhile before they reached a junction. A second shaft now branched to the right, its floor angling downward. The left-hand branch sloped up. Phoenix stopped, holding the torch toward each in turn. Surprisingly, the flame burnt strong and straight toward the left but was almost extinguished by a blast of air from the right.

Hesitating, he looked at the others. "Does it make sense to go *downward* to follow the airflow?"

Jade shrugged. "I'm not getting any more 'feelings' about either direction, so I can't help."

"The waterfall was quite high up," Marcus reminded them.

"Let me send a few lights to the left, just in case." She wafted three foxfires along the upper passage. They stopped about twenty metres along and danced uncertainly in front of a large cave-in. The tunnel was blocked.

"What is it with us and rockfalls?" Brynn muttered.

"OK," Phoenix pointed with the torch, "down it is."

As they descended into the depths of the mountain, a strange, musky scent wafted up the tunnel. The horses reacted to it, jerking back on their reins and whuffling nervously. Jade had to again *command* them into obedience. She laid a hand on the side of her mare's head and closed her eyes for a moment. Opening them, she shook her head.

"I can't understand what's wrong. She's afraid of something, I just can't tell what."

"And you don't get any sense of anything big and nasty up ahead?" Phoenix tried to see beyond the circle of torch-light.

Jade hesitated then tapped her temple with one slender finger. "I…I don't know. It's like there's something blocking me. It feels like my Elven senses are being smothered, somehow. Maybe it's all this rock. I hate being so far inside a mountain." She tugged her cloak closer about her shoulders and gazed upward as if imagining the bulk of the hill over her head.

He laid a hand on her shoulder. "Don't think about it or you'll get claustrophobia. We have enough to worry about already. Let's keep going."

The musky smell got stronger until it made even the humans feel uneasy. It seemed to tweak some primitive instinct in their brains; an instinct that said 'run away!'. Determination and desperation made them ignore it but their hearts raced and sweat beaded on their foreheads as they strained to hear or see invisible dangers ahead.

Distance and time became difficult to judge. Black-and-blood walls slid past without any indication of how far they'd travelled. The tunnel sloped steadily downward. The torch guttered and sputtered in a musk-scented breeze. Hooves clopped on the smooth floor.

Brynn reached out and touched the basalt. "The walls are dry. We must be far enough away from the river."

"The walls are also a lot closer than they were before," Marcus pointed out with a nod.

Jade sent lights ahead. Sure enough, the walls, floor and ceiling were all approaching each other. Even worse, in a few more metres it narrowed to a slender opening through which the horses simply would not fit.

They were stuck.

Once more, it fell to Brynn to slip ahead, into the narrow passage, to scout. When he returned, he shrugged.

"As far as I can tell, it keeps going but the horses are too big, even if we could get them through this." He nodded at the constriction.

"Great," Phoenix groaned. "We can't take them back and we can't take them on. What do we do, leave them here to die?"

"No!" Jade was outraged. Marcus frowned at him.

Phoenix waved them back. "It wasn't a real suggestion. We need ideas. Don't suppose you can transform them into something smaller can you, Jade?"

She shook her head. "You know my magic is limited.

I could cast an *illusion* of smallness but there's no way I could actually change them into something smaller."

"Can you, maybe, *wish* them outside?" He waved his hands in the manner of a Las Vegas magician.

She sent him a scornful glance. "If I could teleport a horse, don't you think I would have just teleported all of us outside?"

"The Bag!" Brynn snapped his fingers. "We survived for at least a day when Jade put us inside the Bag, remember? If we can, so can the horses. We'll put them into the Hyllion Bagia and carry them out."

Phoenix looked at him speculatively. "Will they fit into the opening? I didn't think it was that big."

Jade dragged it out of her pack again and tugged on the drawstring that held the shimmering black material closed. She pulled the cloth experimentally and nodded.

"It's pretty stretchy. If you three hold it and I *command* the horses in, I think it'll work."

She handed the Bag to Marcus. Brynn grabbed at one side and Phoenix a third. Slowly, they backed away from each other, pulling the mouth of the Bag wider and wider until it resembled a huge, black hole suspended horizontally between them. Light fell into it and showed nothing. Jade put a hand in and muttered, 'torch'. Another wooden torch emerged as she withdrew her hand. It still worked.

"Just don't tear it," Brynn warned. "From what I hear about these things, if they get torn, everything inside comes out – all at once. We only know what *we* put into it. It could be hundreds of years old. There could be entire households in there."

Phoenix swallowed and tried to hold the slippery material firmly but gently. "So how do we get the horses to jump in?"

"We don't." Jade made a tilting movement with her hand. "If you turn it vertical, they can walk straight in."

So they did – carefully. Marcus and Phoenix stood on tiptoes to stretch the top as high as they could, while Brynn held the bottom against the floor. Jade firmly *commanded* the horses to walk and they did. Only a certain wildness in their eyes showed their animal instincts fought her magic every stiff step of the way. One by one, the horses and all their gear vanished into the gaping black maw of eerie nothingness.

When it was done, they gingerly turned the hole horizontal again and brought the mouth closed. Tying it shut, Marcus handed it to Jade. She hefted the small, silken thing in one hand, tucked it into her shirt and shook her head in amazement.

"It doesn't even weigh any more than it did. Who would have thought? Good idea, Brynn." She smiled at the boy.

He grinned back at her. "I just hope they don't poop all over my treasure."

Laughing, the four squeezed through the narrow tunnel mouth and continued their downward trek.

Without the unwilling horses, their progress was much faster. The musty scent grew more powerful, until their eyes watered and they coughed from the catch of it in their throats.

"What *is* that smell?" Phoenix demanded, not really expecting an answer. "Can you shield us from it like you did in the sewers in Alexandria, Jade?"

Jade smacked herself in the forehead. "Yes, of course I can. I'm sorry. Here." She muttered a few Elvish words and outlined a circle in the air. Four shimmering, swirling globes of purple-blue light appeared around their heads before fading into a barely-visible distortion.

Brynn took a tentative breath and looked surprised when he realised the air was no longer tainted. "That's amazing!"

Marcus poked gently at the globe, watching with

interest as little sparks and swirls of purple-blue appeared at his fingertip. Brynn followed suit, delighted.

"Just a variation on the shield spell." Jade shrugged but she was clearly pleased by their approval. "It won't keep out weapons, just bad smells and poison gases. If you keep prodding at it, Brynn, it will collapse and I'll have to do it all over again."

He snatched his hand away and sent her a cheeky, guilty grin.

They continued walking and Jade fell in beside Phoenix. "I know I've smelled that scent before," she said, "I just can't think where."

"What about your Elven senses?" He tapped the bubble next to his forehead. "Any luck there?"

She shook her head. "Still nothing. I don't know what I sensed just before the rockfall. It was sort of…like something had just realised we are here and was really angry at us."

"Sweet," he said, mock-cheerfully, "because we needed someone else to be out to get us."

She sighed. "Well, that's what we're here for, isn't it? Beat up the badguys; the henchmen and then the big bad guy - Zhudai. May as well get on with it."

"We're certainly getting lots of practice." He laughed. "You'd think the dudes who wrote this world would have run out of ideas for badguys by now, wouldn't you? I mean, we've had Roman soldiers, trolls, wolves, gods, giants and walking-dead priests. What else can they think up?"

Beneath his feet, Phoenix felt the texture of the floor change. A strange, brittle crunching sound came from under his soles as he strode along the corridor. It felt like he was walking on potato crisps or autumn leaves. Surprised, he looked down.

Beside him, Jade gasped in horror. She turned wide, alarmed eyes on him and gulped. Marcus moved back a pace, his face pale. Brynn stepped up and slapped Phoenix on the shoulder.

"You *had* to ask, didn't you? Well, there's your answer." He pointed at the withered, dried thing that stretched far beyond torchlight, into darkness. Crushed beneath their feet was an impossibly-wide, horrifyingly-long, twisted and desiccated snake skin.

CHAPTER THREE

"Oh," Jade stared at the gruesome relic, "this is really, really not good, is it?"

"Y'think?" Phoenix's sarcasm annoyed her but she ignored it.

"I must admit," Marcus murmured, "I'm not fond of snakes."

His three companions turned to look at their super-cool companion in amazement.

"Did I hear you confess to being afraid of something?" Brynn jibed.

Marcus raised his brows at the youngster. "Only a fool ignores fear. Of course I get scared. I just don't let it paralyse me."

Brynn screwed up his nose as he considered the words. "I'll let you get away with that, I guess." He flashed Marcus a grin and pulled out his sling and dagger. "Shall we keep going?"

Jade groaned. "Do we have a choice?"

"After you, oh great leader." Brynn bowed mockingly toward Phoenix.

Phoenix didn't respond but swatted the boy lightly on the back of the head as he passed by. Unfazed, Brynn snickered.

Behind them, Jade fell into step with Marcus, her staff held ready. They had gone perhaps another thirty or forty metres when she stopped and grabbed Marcus' arm.

"Wait," she called.

Phoenix and Brynn turned back.

"I hear something," she explained as they looked at her. Her half-Elven hearing was better than a human's so they all waited as she concentrated on sorting out the faint noises.

"It's echoing oddly but I think…I think it's voices," she finally said, surprised. "Oh!" A new noise spiked so loudly that the others heard it, too. "That was a sword hitting rock. Someone's in trouble."

"Let's go then!" Phoenix turned on his heel and jogged away, carrying their torch like an Olympic runner.

The others exchanged looks and began to hurry after him, trusting in Jade's dim lights to show the way.

"So why are we running *toward* a fight?" Brynn panted when they caught up.

Phoenix glanced down at him, laying a hand on Blódbál and grinning. "It's what we do best?"

Brynn sent him a sardonic look that spoke volumes. "So how will we know who's friend and who's foe?"

"He has a point." Loping easily beside the boy, Marcus was barely out of breath as he spoke.

Phoenix shrugged. "Let's just get there first and hide. We'll work it out."

Jade had to bite her tongue to stop herself commenting on his tendency to jump in without planning. With Blódbál singing songs of glorious, heroic death in his head, it'd be impossible to make him stop and strategise instead.

They ran on, their footfalls reflecting back sharp slaps off the rock walls. The clamour of fierce battle grew louder. Cries of at least two people mingled with other, strangely-sibilant, sounds – all weirdly distorted by the tunnels. Whoever fought, they sounded desperate. Sword strikes rang with bell-like clarity through the rock, echoing until it sounded like a dozen swordsmen striking in quick succession. The companions picked up their pace, running recklessly along the straight passageway.

The tunnel took a sharp left and they skidded around, barely managing to avoid crashing into the wall and each other. Ahead, a massive, archway marked the end of the tunnel and the entrance to a large, dimly-lit chamber beyond. Jade doused her lights and the torch. On silent feet, they edged up to the entryway and peered around.

Beside her, Jade felt Marcus stiffen and heard him choke back an involuntary cry. She didn't blame him. It was all she could do to stop herself from gasping aloud at the sight.

A huge, vaulted cavern lay before them. They had emerged on the lowest level. Above, the curving walls were honeycombed with dark, gaping entrances like the one in which they sheltered. A few, smouldering torches cast a flickering, ruddy light in patches here and there but there was more darkness than illumination. At one end stood a pair of massive thrones, carved from the rock itself. On those thrones reclined a king and queen unlike any Jade had ever imagined.

Glittering crowns of gold and jewels rested in stately fashion upon handsome human heads. The heads rested upon perfect human shoulders and torsos. Below that, though, was the stuff of nightmares. Curled up on the throne seats were not legs but massive, mottled snake-bodies. The king and queen were half-human, half-snake.

That was not the worst. In front of the throne lay a real snake so huge it defied belief. Its thick, blue-grey body coiled three times around the thrones. The twitching tip of its tail rested in the lap of the snake king. Its blunt head, the size of a washing machine, swayed, hood expanded, tongue flickering as it stared fixedly toward the middle of the throne room.

Jade followed the cobra's gaze and saw two humans fighting fiercely against more snake-men. The humans were armed with short broadswords and daggers. Not only did the snake-warriors wield lethally-sharp sinuous blades in each hand, they also bared long, poison-tipped fangs. Forked tongues flicked each time they hissed at their victims. They moved with gliding ease across the smooth rock floor. More and more of them swarmed toward the beleaguered humans. The warriors fought valiantly but sheer force of numbers would soon overwhelm them.

"I think we can guess who's friend and who's foe," Brynn whispered. "Any plans?"

"Jade?" Phoenix didn't take his eyes off the room.

She nibbled the tip of one finger, frowning. It always seemed to fall to her to come up with some sort of brilliant plan. She studied the situation, trying to ignore the nervous self-doubt fluttering in her stomach.

"They seem to be trying to get over to that exit." She pointed at the far end of the throne room, about thirty metres from their own hiding place. Indeed, the two humans were doing their level best to hew a way through the reptilian bodies to get to one, specific door.

"Maybe that's the way they came in – and the way out," Marcus suggested.

Phoenix nodded. "Worth a try. Can you even the odds, Jade? Marcus and I are good but we'll still be outnumbered."

She bit her lip. "I can't blind them the way I did the Priests of Set, because that would blind the humans, too. Besides, snakes can 'see' by scent so they'd probably be fine without vision."

"How about an illusion? But make it fast. I don't think they have much time."

"OK," she agreed. "I'll send in the cavalry and we'll use it as cover to rescue them. Hopefully they can lead us out of here. What do snakes hate?"

"Cats?" "Dogs?" "Eagles?" "Ferrets?" The suggestions came quickly.

Brynn blinked at Phoenix. "What's a ferret?"

"It's kind of like a weasel," Jade explained, "but here in India it's called a mongoose. How about we send all of them in? Give me a few seconds. It's going to take a lot of concentration, though. I won't be able to fight."

"Brynn, you stay with Jade and lead her around the edge of the room to that exit. Protect her as best you can." Phoenix gave the boy's shoulder a squeeze.

Brynn nodded, loading a small rock into his sling and hefting his dagger.

A cry of pain from one of the humans echoed around the chamber. He staggered and his companion caught him up, still fighting one-handed as the snake-people closed in. Phoenix growled low in his throat. His fingers tightened on his sword. If she wasn't fast, he'd dash out on his own and fall under the spell of the blade's desire for blood.

Quickly, she muttered an Elvish incantation, picturing the animals in her mind. Beside her, Brynn yelped as the illusory zoo streamed silently out into the chamber. Belatedly, she added noise and substance to the images.

All hell broke loose.

A cacophony of yowls, barks, screelings and weird yelpings assaulted their ears. The snake-men recoiled in fear at the sight of a hundred, larger-than-life predators galloping and flying toward them. Every shape, colour and size of cat, dog, ferret and eagle Jade could imagine bore down on the enemy with fangs and claws bared.

Under cover of the chaos, Phoenix and Marcus dashed out to join the human fighters, slicing their way through.

Jade hardly felt Brynn grab her hand and lead her into the chamber. It took most of her attention to keep up such a detailed illusion. He squeezed her hand as they crept from shadow to shadow along the wall.

"Why are there more eagles now?" he whispered, apparently fascinated by the show. Sure enough, the number of birds clawing and shrieking at the snakemen had doubled but there were fewer dogs.

"It's what they're most afraid of. The more they believe, the stronger the illusions get." Jade said through clenched teeth. "Their fear is feeding power to the spell. If they're scared enough, the illusion can actually hurt them – it's psychological."

"Syco-what?" Brynn deftly flung a small pebble with his sling, knocking one snake-man unconscious.

"Can we talk about this later? This is hard enough to do without you distracting me. Just get us out of here!" Jade gripped her long, wooden staff, hoping she wouldn't need to use it. Energy drained from her body like water, pouring into the illusions.

She spared the others a quick look. Phoenix and Marcus reached the two humans and entered the fray enthusiastically. With Blódbál in hand and Marcus watching his back, Phoenix looked unstoppable. The only thing they really had to worry about was being bitten by one of the snakemen. Both of the other warriors were on their feet again, although the wounded one, an older man, looked shaken. With a quick nod of acknowledgement to the newcomers, they closed ranks and struck out at the enemy.

Jade kept half an eye on Phoenix as he slashed at a snake tail, cleaving it in two. Its owner shrieked and fell over, thrashing on the ground. Two of his companions dragged him aside, leaving a temporary gap in the wall of bodies. The humans used it to gain a few more precious steps towards the exit.

A raucous cry from above made the two strangers flinch but Phoenix and Marcus stayed focussed. They must have realised it was just her illusion eagles. Sure enough, three birds soared down, claws raking and wings battering at the faces of the enemy. Brynn's handy sling took down another snake-man slithering up behind Marcus.

Blódbál bit deeply into reptile flesh, its unholy blood-lust reflected in Phoenix's face. Jade gasped as Phoenix barely avoided a wild sword-thrust. He grabbed the snake-man's hand and jerked it forward, using his enemy's own forward momentum to bring him within striking distance. Blódbál slid between ribs without a sound and the half-reptile gaped in shock before slipping to the ground, dead.

She heard Brynn choke back a warning as yet another enemy tried to sneak up on Phoenix from behind. Somehow he saw, snatched out his dagger, and managed to turn aside a blade aimed at his head. Striking low, Blódbál connected. His expression grew harder. The light of battle flamed in his eyes. He shook his head as though trying to shake the sword's song from it. Jade wondered if he would give in to it and strike out at Marcus and the others.

A quick glance showed Phoenix's three fighting companions also still on their feet and at his side. The exit was closer but there seemed to be an unending supply of the enemy. Metre by metre, the four fought their way toward the tunnel, leaving a bloody trail of wounded and dying snake-warriors behind.

Steel rang on steel. Sibilant, hissing screams and triumphant eagle-cries tore the air. Stone after stone from Brynn's sling caught snake-men in the head with deadly accuracy. Phoenix's arm was a blur of movement as he sliced, turned, sliced, jabbed and hacked at the enemy without mercy. Marcus fought coolly at his back, his expression grim and determined. From the nearby shadows, Jade dared to think they might actually make it.

Brynn tugged at her arm and pointed. She glanced up. Emerging from many of the tunnel openings overhead were dozens more snake-men. They slid and groped their way down to the floor before rearing up on those muscular tails and heading for the fight. There was no way the human warriors could possibly defeat that many, illusions and magic swords or not.

Reaching a quick decision, Jade focussed her thoughts on two of the eagles, making them split off from the massive flock that now soared about the chamber. With a frown of concentration, she sent them arrowing straight at the king and queen of the snake-people. The huge golden birds shrieked and dove, vicious claws extended, right toward exposed faces.

As she'd hoped, the royal pair cried out in fear and flung up their arms. The eagles raked them, leaving long, red welts before flying off to circle around and attack again. The enormous cobra at their feet hissed and struck at the diving birds, missing. With their king and queen in immediate danger, over half of the warriors attacking Phoenix and Marcus slithered away. Jade sent the eagles in again and again, feeling ill as the curving claws and beaks tore at snakeman flesh and skin. Obviously snake-people feared eagles more than anything and their fear gave the illusion real power. The claw-wounds were deep and bloody. More warriors left the fight and went to help their leaders.

Brynn shook her arm. "We've made it to the exit and so have the others. Quick. C'mon."

Jade took one last look at the chaos of the throneroom. The eagles she'd created were now so solid that they had taken on a life of their own. They were no longer her illusions: they were real animals, given life by the power of belief. Swooping and diving at the snake-men, hundreds continued to cause havoc, covering the escape of the humans. Marcus, Phoenix and the other two ran past, sweeping Brynn along with them into the tunnel exit.

She glanced at the thrones, feeling a twinge of regret for so many deaths. More and more eagles winged toward the royal couple. A forest of waving swords sprang up around them, trying to prevent more diving attacks. None of the snake-men bothered to chase her friends any longer. It was time to make a getaway.

As she turned to leave, an island of stillness in the midst of so much frantic movement caught her eye. The enormous snake, coiled at the kings' feet, now stared in her direction, its black gaze turned, unblinking on her. One soulless eye fixed on Jade as she stood in the tunnel entrance. Its large head lifted higher, the hood expanded, tongue flickering out toward her as though tasting her scent.

Once more a sudden foreboding took hold of her, followed by a sense of extreme anger and a merciless desire for revenge. The eye seemed to grow larger, as though the great snake had crossed the room and entered into her mind without moving a muscle. Darkness descended. The throne room and everything in it disappeared. All she could see was that eye. Jade swallowed hard, trying to turn her head, trying to break the connection. Sweat broke out on her forehead but she couldn't move a muscle; couldn't even blink.

Her whole body trembled in an effort to fight the cobra's mental hold over her. Against her will, her hand opened and the oaken staff she cherished clattered to the ground. She tried to open her mouth and cry for help but nothing happened. Then, slowly, her leg began to shake. She took a small step, and another; and another. It felt as though she had run a marathon. Her heart thundered in her chest.

She took another step, longer than before; and another.

The only problem was: each step took her *toward* the snake, not away from it.

CHAPTER FOUR

Phoenix sprinted out into the open air right on the heels of the two warriors. Dusk had crept in to replace daylight. Pink and orange flares set fire to high clouds as a hazy red sun slipped behind the mountains. In the east, the sky deepened to rich purples.

Hoping they knew where they were going, Phoenix followed the warriors when they took an abrupt turn to the right and headed for a nearby clump of trees. Behind, he heard heavy footfalls and harsh breathing. Since the snakemen had no feet, it was safe to assume the sounds were made by Marcus and the others.

Risking a quick look, he was relieved to see a complete absence of reptiles. Seconds later, he skidded to a halt, his boots spraying up dirt and dust. Marcus swerved to miss him but Brynn couldn't stop in time and ploughed headfirst into Phoenix's stomach.

Gasping for breath, he shoved the boy aside. "Where's Jade?"

Marcus and Brynn looked back. She wasn't there.

"She was right behind me," Brynn exclaimed.

"Well she's not now. Let's go get her."

"What about them?" Marcus jerked his chin at the still-fleeing humans they'd rescued.

Phoenix shook his head. "We don't have time to ask them. C'mon."

Even as they began to run back toward the towering

black mountain, they heard hurried steps behind. One of the warriors returned. He caught them up with easy, long strides.

"Your friend?"

Phoenix nodded. "She's still in there."

"Llew is wounded. He's getting our horses. I'll help you." The man drew his sword again and they all plunged back into the dark tunnel.

Inside, they were forced to slow down. Without Jade's guiding lights, the darkness was almost complete. Luckily, the tunnel was quite short and their new companion seemed to know which direction to take. He advanced without hesitation, sword ready. Soon, a faint, reddish light appeared and they approached the main chamber.

At the tunnel opening, they flattened themselves against the shadowed walls and peered inside. Chaos still reigned. Jade's flock of eagles battered and clawed at the snakemen but several pathetic piles of feathers on the floor showed the battle was balancing out. Most of the snakemen were busy protecting their king and queen.

"What is she doing?" Brynn whispered.

Jade was about ten steps away, walking slowly and jerkily toward the thrones. Her staff lay near to the tunnel, abandoned.

Phoenix shook his head. "Stupid question. She's obviously lost her mind."

The stranger nudged him and pointed at the great snake coiled at the base of the thrones. Its head was lifted off the floor, its eyes fixed on Jade.

"I think you might be right. There are rumours that the Naga snake-goddess, Manasa Devi, can control people's minds. I think your friend is under her spell."

A dozen questions popped into Phoenix's head but he decided to leave them for a more quiet time – whenever that might be.

"So we just go out and pick her up." He took a step

forward.

"No," the stranger reached out to hold him back. "Manasa will make her fight us with everything she's got. Either she'll die or we will."

Phoenix exchanged unhappy looks with the others. None of them wanted to face Jade throwing 'everything' at them. She had learned spells from that Svear wizard that none of them had even seen yet. There was no knowing of what she was truly capable.

"So how do we get her back?" Marcus demanded.

"Like this." The newcomer drew a leaf-shaped knife from a belt slung across his chest. It was one of a dozen sheathed there. Expertly, he flipped it over until it lay, point-forward, flat on his palm and fingers. He pulled his arm back to throw.

Phoenix frowned, judging the distance between them and the snake. It was over forty metres away. "There's no way you can…" he began.

The warrior threw with a soft grunt of effort. The knife flew through the air like a bullet, soaring straight toward the snake. A second later, the blade embedded itself up to the hilt in the cobra's eye. A vast shriek of despair went up from the snake-people. The king leapt from his throne and wrapped his arms around the thrashing snake-head, holding the animal still. Tears streamed down his face.

Jade stopped walking. She stood for a second, swaying in time to the movements of the great snake's body. Then she crumpled to the ground, unconscious.

Swearing, the strange warrior dashed out of cover with Phoenix, Marcus and Brynn close behind. In one swift move, he scooped Jade up in his arms and flung her limp body over a broad shoulder. Spinning, he sprinted back toward the exit. Phoenix followed, choking on the overpowering smell of musk now that Jade's shield air-filter had vanished. Gasping, he grabbed her staff and trailed behind with the others, feeling inadequate and angry.

A great, sobbing and wailing arose in the cave. The sound followed them, echoing hauntingly in the tunnels as they made their escape a second time. Beneath their feet, the earth shuddered. Small pieces of rock clattered and dropped around them. As they burst into open air again, a great rumbling sounded overhead. The companions picked up their pace, lungs straining for air as they raced to put distance between them and the mountain. Finally, the shaking and rumbling ceased and all was still.

It was almost full dark. Phoenix turned and looked back at the mountain. The tunnel entrance was gone – completely covered by an enormous landslide that had taken a huge bite out of the slope above. Dust wafted through the evening air. High above, a faint eagle-shriek echoed through the valley.

"Again with the rockfalls," Brynn said.

The stranger appeared not to hear the comment. "We need to keep moving. That won't hold the Naga for long and I don't think they'll be happy about what we've done today. Do you have horses nearby?"

Phoenix looked sideways at Jade's limp form, thinking fast. "Yes. How about you go find your friend and make sure he's ok, while we get our horses."

"We'll meet by the river and head downstream toward the village of Paud." The warrior pointed east.

Phoenix shrugged, not wanting to get into an argument. "Sounds fine. See you in a minute."

The man lowered Jade into Marcus' arms and nodded. Turning, he jogged away into the gathering gloom.

Jade stirred, groaning. Marcus placed her carefully on the ground and ran an expert eye over her. "She doesn't appear to be injured."

Phoenix slapped her lightly on the cheek. "Wake up, Jade. We need the Bag."

Marcus frowned at him and Brynn let out a wordless protest.

"Wha…?" Her eyelids fluttered and she stared vaguely at them for a moment before sense returned. She sat up, looking around with wild fear. "The snake!"

"It's ok," Phoenix assured her, "you're safe outside but we need the horses to get away fast. Give me the Bag."

"Oh, yes." With a shaking hand, she withdrew the Hyllion Bagia from inside her shirt and handed it to him.

Phoenix, Brynn and Marcus stretched it out. Jade climbed slowly to her feet and reached inside. In rapid succession five, very disorientated, horses clopped out of nothingness, into the night air. Phoenix returned the Bag to Jade, who tucked it away and hauled herself into the saddle.

"Which way to the river?" he demanded.

She closed her eyes and pointed northeast. Her whole body trembled. He was worried about her but they didn't have time to talk. They had to put as much distance between them and the mountain as possible. If these two strangers knew their way around, as they seemed to, then they would be useful as guides to the village. She could recover there.

With Jade's wordless directions to guide them, they reached the river in just a few minutes. Two horsemen emerged from the deep shadow of a tree.

"Well met," came the voice of the man who'd saved Jade. "I'm Cadoc. This is Llew. Our thanks for a timely rescue."

"And ours for your rescue of our companion," Phoenix replied cordially. He introduced himself and the others before getting back to more important matters. "Can you lead us to this village?"

"Of course. You mean you didn't come up the valley to get here?" Cadoc turned his horse and kicked it into a fast walk.

"No," Phoenix replied, not wishing to get into details

of their strange mode of travel from Level to Level in this world.

Oddly, Cadoc didn't ask any more questions. He did, however, jump in shock when a dozen little green witchlights appeared in midair before them.

"Sorry," Jade murmured. "I should have warned you. They're mine."

Cadoc edged his horse alongside hers and bowed in her direction. "You're a Spellweaver, my lady?"

"Yes." Her reply was even quieter than before.

Phoenix was alarmed to see her sway in the saddle. Her lights dimmed.

Cadoc reached out and steadied her. "Be brave, my lady. It's but a short ride to safety. The Naga rarely venture close to the village."

"Thankyou," Jade managed. "How is your friend?" She nodded at the other rider.

Cadoc grinned, his teeth white in the darkness. "Llew is strong. He took a blade in the shoulder that was meant for me but the blood is staunched. He will fight again."

The group rode on in silence, listening for sounds of pursuit. Only the sighing of a breeze in the nearby forest and the splashy gurgle of the shallow river reached their straining ears. Overhead, stars flickered and glimmered through the last dusty purple hues of sunset. Crickets sang in the darkness.

Although that night-ride seemed to last for many hours, Phoenix later realised it took less than one from the time they escaped the mountain to the moment they trudged wearily into the small village of Paud.

There were no more than forty houses, scattered around a packed-earth open central area. Mostly wood, bamboo and thatching, the houses straggled along either side of narrow dirt paths and sprinkled up into the surrounding hills. Many were dark but here and there the smoky red of hearth fires glowed through open doors.

As the sound of hooves echoed between the buildings, curious brown faces peered at the travellers from all sides. Hushed whispers drifted out of the darkness. Then, with a cry of recognition, the door of the largest house in town flew open and an elderly man hurried out. Barefoot and dressed only in what looked like a long piece of cloth wrapped like a diaper around his hips and legs, the man jogged spryly out to meet them. With a gap-toothed grin, he pressed his hands together and bowed.

"Namaste. Namaste. You are back! We did not believe you would return from that place so soon. Did you meet with Manasa and Vasuki?"

Cadoc smiled down at the old man and shook his head. He looked across at Phoenix with a rueful shrug. "I have no idea what he's saying. I think he's speaking Sanskrit. They were kind to us on our way up here and he seems glad we're back."

Phoenix blinked at him in confusion. What did he mean, he couldn't understand the old Indian? It was perfectly clear. Comprehension dawned: the spell Ásúlfr had cast on them in Svealand. The old wizard had given them all the gift of understanding any language. Phoenix had become so used to the ability, he no longer thought about it. Cadoc, of course, didn't have the skill. He had spoken to them in the Breton language and they had all answered without even thinking.

"He is glad," Phoenix supplied. "He's saying he didn't expect you back so soon."

Llew and Cadoc stared at him in surprise then Cadoc smiled. "Now I'm doubly pleased we have met. Travelling without being able to speak the language of the natives has been challenging. Please tell him we are happy to be back amongst friends."

Phoenix translated and the old man grinned at him, nodded and bowed deeply.

"I am Samir. Please, come, you are all welcome in

Paud. Come, come. You will stay with me." He swept a hand toward his house. A small boy appeared to hold the reins of their horses as the travellers dismounted.

"I'll see to the horses." Marcus led their five animals away as the boy tugged other two toward the back of the house.

Jade staggered as she slid to the ground. Phoenix, who was closest, grabbed her elbow and held her up. Brynn slipped under her other arm. She sent both of them a grateful, weary smile. Cadoc supported Llew and all five followed the old man into the house.

Inside, a white-haired Indian woman, dressed in a red sari, fussed as they entered. She scolded Samir ruthlessly, not even pausing when he introduced her as Leela, his wife. Two younger women, also wearing vibrantly-coloured saris, went quietly about the business of helping their guests. Llew and Jade were led off to simple bedrooms while Phoenix, Cadoc and Brynn were ushered into a small kitchen area. Marcus joined them moments later.

Leela bustled around the room, cooking a simple meal of flatbreads and vegetables on an open hearth. Samir showed his guests to a low table and bade them sit on woven mats. He served them water in basic pottery cups and ordered his daughters to bring more water to wash in.

Phoenix touched one of the girls on the arm. "Where is my friend, the girl?"

She looked at him with large, dark eyes and bowed. "She is sleeping, master. Mother says she will be well in the morning. The man needs a shaman for his shoulder but he is away in the next village. Mother says she will send someone to fetch him in the morning."

"I should check on him. He's an old servant of my family." Cadoc excused himself and followed Samir's daughter into the back of the house.

Phoenix turned back to their host. The old Indian smiled encouragingly at Brynn, who struggled to scoop a thick paste of vegetables and yellowish sauce onto a chapatti flatbread. Phoenix watched, amused, as Brynn took a cautious bite. The boy chewed and swallowed, opening his eyes in surprise at the new flavours. Then his eyes began to water. His mouth opened and he let out a faint mew of distress. Sticking out his tongue, he waved a hand at it, breathing quickly.

"Hot! Hot! Hot!" He snatched at a cup of water and downed it in one gulp, sputtering and choking. Eyes streaming, he sniffed and wiped his nose on his sleeve. Turning an outraged expression on Phoenix, he pointed at the food. "They're trying to poison us!"

Samir and Leela dissolved into giggles. Phoenix tried to keep a straight face but failed, laughed and shook his head.

"It's just spices, Brynn. It's perfectly safe. Try the yoghurt." He indicated a bowl on the table.

Brynn eyed it suspiciously but scooped some onto a piece of chapatti and ate it. Looking relieved, he mixed some with a second bit of curry and managed to swallow with more dignity, though his eyes still watered.

Cadoc returned to say Llew and Jade both slept. The exhausted group ate in silence, bid their kind host and hostess goodnight and went to do the same.

Phoenix awoke early feeling surprisingly refreshed. Easing himself up from his floor-mat at first light, he dressed quietly so as not to disturb Marcus and Brynn. He strapped on his weapons and pushed aside the door-curtain, intending to check on Jade. Stepping out into the narrow hallway, he almost collided with Cadoc and Llew.

Now, in the light of day, Phoenix felt a twinge of something horribly like envy as he saw exactly how like the ideal hero Cadoc appeared. The stranger looked, perhaps, a year or two older than Phoenix's avatar and every inch the gentleman-warrior. Tall and muscular, with grey eyes and thick, dark blond hair, he had charisma and charm, as well as amazing good looks. He wore a shirt, vest and trousers of fine cloth. His sword, throwing knives and dagger were of the best metal and he carried himself with the air of someone used to being a leader of men.

Phoenix nodded politely and gestured for the two men to precede him toward the front door. Cadoc supported Llew, who staggered as he moved forward. Together, the three stepped out into the balmy morning and blinked in the soft yellow light. Cadoc helped the older man to sit on a narrow wooden log bench in front of the house. Then he stood, scrubbed a hand through his thick hair and stretched with a sinew-cracking yawn.

Phoenix gasped, staring at the embroidery that decorated the fine linen cloth of the man's shirt beneath the vest. It was a single letter: *P*.

"You're a Player!" he breathed, stunned. "The game is open."

CHAPTER FIVE

Cadoc sent him a quizzical smile and nodded at the same letter emblazoned on Phoenix's leather arm guard. "You too, I see. What a bizarre thing to say. Of course the game's open. It's been open for about eight hours now."

Phoenix could only stare at him, shell-shocked. Only eight hours! They had been inside 80AD almost two weeks but when they had left the real world, the game was still two days away from being live. So in two weeks here, only a little over two days had passed in the real world.

He was still trying to get his head around the differences in the passage of time when another, more unwelcome thought occurred. If the game was open to everyone, would they be swamped with other Players seeking to defeat Zhudai as well? If someone else killed the warlock, would they still be able to get home? Questions he couldn't easily ask spun through his head.

Realising Cadoc still watched him, Phoenix pulled himself together and tried to ask something easy. "Llew's your Companion?"

Cadoc shrugged, frowning as his friend coughed painfully.

"Llew has been a servant of my avatar's family for many years." He turned to survey the small village. "Come, let's walk and leave Llew to soak up the sun awhile."

Forgetting his earlier wish to check on Jade, Phoenix

turned to walk beside the Player as he strolled along the dirt road.

"What about you? Which of your friends is your Companion? I thought you could only have one." Cadoc sent him a swift, sideways look.

"Jade and I are both Players," he admitted. "Brynn and Marcus are our friends."

"Both Players?" Cadoc's expression turned briefly puzzled then faintly worried. "How does that work? How long have you been travelling together?"

They reached the centre of the village and watched Paud coming to life. Women chattered as they walked toward the river with their hips swaying. Tall water containers, balanced on their heads, remained perfectly still. Bright saris contrasted strikingly with warm, dark skin and long, black hair. Laughter and the twitter of birds floated through the clear air.

Small children jogged alongside or played games in the dust at their mothers' feet. A boy about Brynn's age drove a small herd of sheep out of a pen and headed for mountain pastures. Several men of the village walked past, bare-chested and wearing the wrapped-cloth shorts Phoenix now knew were called 'dhoti'. They called out greetings and Cadoc waved back. An armband studded with seven rubies glittered on his upper arm. Five of them were dull and lifeless.

Phoenix saw no harm in answering his questions – in a limited way. It wouldn't do to tell him he was more than just a digital construct of this fake game-world. He'd never believe it anyway. He chose his words carefully.

"We met the first time we both started Playing. Since we had the same goals to achieve, we figured we might as well work together."

Cadoc stared at him in astonishment. "You both have the same Quest? I thought that was impossible."

"Huh?" Now it was Phoenix's turn to stare.

"The game rules clearly state that every Player has an individual Quest. It's written that way precisely to stop people from getting groups together and making an army of Players. The programmers must have stuffed up. I can't believe your luck." He shook his head.

Phoenix gulped. It was just one more piece of evidence that showed exactly how unique their situation was. Obviously their coming into this game was no accident; but how had it happened and who had orchestrated it? How had they circumvented the programming to give him and Jade the same quest if everyone else had different ones? At least they didn't have to worry about someone else finishing off Zhudai. Or was that a bad thing?

"So what's your task on this Level?" he asked, trying to maintain some sort of normal conversation after that bombshell.

Cadoc held up a hand and glanced around cautiously. "We're really not supposed to talk about it. Didn't you hear what happened to that guy in America?"

"Uh," Phoenix groped for an answer, "no. I haven't been onto any chat sites lately." That was an understatement. He'd almost forgotten what a computer even looked like – from the outside anyway.

"The programmers caught him talking in-game about his Quest and his real-world life. They deleted him and banned him from the game." Cadoc frowned.

"Deleted…" Phoenix clutched the hilt of his sword.

He took a deep breath and let it go slowly. OK, so that was the final nail in the coffin of the 'contact-the-outside-world' idea. Getting another Player to help or deliver a message was clearly out of the question. If they all had different Quests and no-one could talk about the outside world then no-one would want to help them. If Cadoc was telling the truth then it was all the more reason not to reveal how he and Jade came to be here, together. They were on their own until they completed the game.

Shaken, Phoenx spun on his heel. "I need to go check on Jade." Ignoring Cadoc's surprised look, he hurried back to the house. He had to talk to Jade before she went blabbing to Cadoc or Llew.

*****

Jade woke slowly, feeling battered and empty. Her limbs hung heavy and her neck was stiff. Opening her eyes, she stared blankly at a bamboo wall for several seconds with no idea at all of where she was. It came back in a rush and she sat up. The mountain-cave; the giant cobra; the village of Paud.

The memory of the snake's mind entwined with her own set her stomach roiling. She grabbed a bowl that sat conveniently beside her sleeping mat. With a deep shudder, she threw up into it. Since she'd eaten nothing, nothing much came out but she felt a little better anyway. Putting the bowl down, she took a swallow of tepid water from her waterskin and swilled it around in her mouth before spitting it out.

She pulled up her legs, wrapped her arms around them and rested her head on her knees. The snake had been in complete control of her body. She'd felt so helpless. A few more seconds would have put her within striking distance of those long, venomous fangs. If Cadoc and the others hadn't come back for her, there was no telling what might have happened. It wasn't really the thought of dying – again – that made Jade uneasy. It was the memory of being powerless; of having no control over her body and mind. She hugged her knees tighter, trying to think about something else.

A slight sound nearby made her snatch at her dagger in alarm. Cadoc slipped into the room and crouched nearby, watching her with concern in his clear grey eyes. Jade sniffed defiantly and scrubbed a hand across her cheeks, feeling them flame with embarrassment. In the light of day, he was even more handsome than she'd realised.

Holding out a steaming cup, he smiled at her. "Here, Leela sent you some tea. Feeling any better today?"

Jade nodded and ran hasty fingers through her tangled hair with one hand as she took the cup with the other. She must look an absolute fright. Scrambling to her feet, she swayed as a wave of dizziness hit. Cadoc's strong fingers gripped her elbow.

"Take it easy," he sounded concerned, "you had a rough day yesterday."

She sighed and took a sip of the fragrant brew. "You can say that again."

"It's not every day you get a snake-goddess in your head and live to tell the story." He grinned at her.

She laughed reluctantly. "Well, actually, life's been pretty hectic lately. So far hardly a day has passed without some god trying to kill me. I'm kinda getting used to it. Ummm…thanks for saving me."

Cadoc shook his head. "Not a problem. Just returning the favour. Always glad to help a beautiful maiden in distress."

Flattered, Jade smiled shyly at him. She suddenly began to wish for all the things she'd never cared about before – makeup, hair dryers, pretty clothes. Patting her hair again self-consciously, she backed away a little; stumbling over her sleeping mat.

"Umm… maybe I should tidy up and we can talk over breakfast."

"I'll look forward to it. I must go help Llew. He wants to go out in the sun this morning." He turned to go.

"Oh! Wait," she called. "How is he?"

He frowned. "He's hiding it well but I think the wound is troubling him more than it should. He's not a young man any more."

"Would you," she began, "I mean… I could heal it if you like."

"You can?" Cadoc sent her an admiring look that made her blush. "I would be grateful. Llew is a good servant and shield-mate. While I have a couple of lives to spare, he doesn't and I'd hate to think his decision to protect me could prove fatal. I'll give you a few minutes to tidy up and then I'll bring him in."

He bowed and had left the room before the significance of his comment sank into Jade's befuddled brain.

A couple of lives? Cadoc had a couple of lives to spare? That meant… Her hand crept to her mouth in astonishment. For several long minutes she stood, staring into space, considering the implications of what he had said. Finally, she shook herself, sipped again at the rapidly-cooling tea and took care of a few morning necessities.

A short time later, Phoenix burst into the room without ceremony as she rummaged in her pack for clean clothes. He grabbed her arm and gave her a slight shake.

"Jade, be careful what you say to Cadoc and Llew," he warned. "Cadoc's-"

"A Player," she pulled free and rubbed her arm, "I know. Why should that stop me from talking to them? Surely it means we can get a message home like we hoped?"

"No!" he almost shouted then glanced upward like he was afraid someone could hear. "No. Cadoc said Players are all supposed to have different Quests. Anyone who talks in-game about the quests or about their real-world lives gets…deleted. Just be careful what you say."

She gaped at him in horror and glanced at the door, wondering if she'd said anything wrong to Cadoc. No, their conversation hadn't even touched on quests or real lives. Relieved that she hadn't endangered her new friend or herself, she was more abrupt with Phoenix than she meant to be.

"I'm not stupid, you know," she said coolly. "Now would you mind? I need to help Llew."

He sent her a quick, hurt look and strode out, brushing past Cadoc who led Llew down the corridor.

Entering the room, Cadoc glanced back over his shoulder at Phoenix's retreating back. "Is he alright?"

Jade shrugged. "He's just being bossy. He'll get over it. Now, let's see what we've got. Lie down."

Llew sent her a grateful, exhausted smile and sank onto the sleeping mat with a sigh and a cough. Blood spotted his lips. He winced as she eased his vest off and slid his shirt down off his left shoulder.

She sucked in a long, hissing breath at the sight of the ugly wound. Leela's daughters had packed it well with wadded cloth but blood had seeped through and crusted the cloth onto his skin. It must have hurt when it came off but he barely uttered a sound. Grimacing, she looked at the man properly for the first time and found him gazing back at her with solemn, pained dark eyes. He smiled, creases forming in his weatherbeaten skin. Reaching out with his right hand, he gripped her fingers weakly.

"You are as kind as you are beautiful, my lady. Thank you for trying to help me but I fear it may be too late. Please, look after my master."

Jade blinked at the older man in dismay, wondering if he were right. She had to try, though. Cadoc obviously thought highly of him and she didn't want to let her new friend down. She pressed her lips together and shook her head, saying briskly, "Don't be silly. You'll be fine."

Sitting back on her heels, she took stock of her own inner resources. She'd spent a week in the lifeless deserts of Egypt and it had taken a toll. Hers was an earthy magic; linked to nature and the life of the forest. Drawing a deep breath, she smelled the rich scents of warm, fertile earth, water and plants. Deep in her bones, she felt the presence of living trees and drew some strength from them as she did back in England. They 'tasted' slightly different in her mind but their essential earth-connection was the same. Magic had been difficult in the dry deserts of Egypt. Here it should be easier. The question was: did she have enough left to perform a difficult Healing?

First she mixed a few herbs together with a little water and pressed them to the torn flesh. Then, closing her eyes, Jade reached out and laid her hand on Llew's shoulder. Murmuring the Elvish healing spell, she allowed power to flow through her palm. Frowning, she 'felt' the wound; knitting torn muscle; repairing a severed vein; reconnecting a broken tendon. It was a more complex injury than any she'd had to deal with so far. The blade had entered and twisted as it came out, leaving a ragged, deep cut. It had nicked an artery and the top of the left lung, too. She had to repair that and drain the blood slowly filling Llew's vital airways. She also detected snake-venom that would need to be destroyed before it affected any organs. The healing was a delicate, difficult task and it took far more energy than she'd planned.

Then, when it was almost complete, his heart stopped.

Aloud, Jade yelled "No!" and poured everything she had into the effort. Gritting her teeth, she sent a massive shock into Llew's body in an effort to re-start his heart. The world began to spin as she sat back and tried to focus on her patient. She lost the connection with him. Did his heart beat? Worried, she reached for the yin-yang amulet around her neck; hoping to draw power from it as she had in Egypt. Her arms were too heavy. They wouldn't move. She was so tired. So very, very tired. Perhaps if she just slept for awhile, she would feel better. Sliding onto the floor beside Llew, she barely heard Brynn's frightened cry before the world vanished into darkness.

*****

Phoenix, Marcus and Brynn entered Jade's room in time to watch the last few seconds of the healing. Jade crouched over the warrior with her eyes closed and a deep frown creasing her forehead. Her right hand hovered over the wounded shoulder. An intense, purple-blue glow shimmered beneath her palm, arcing and crackling around Llew's shoulder. It seemed to slide beneath his skin, lighting his body from the inside as her magic cleansed and cured the deep wound.

Her eyes flew open, vividly green against the bruises of tiredness beneath them. She gasped a single, strangled "No!". The glow at her fingers flashed into a blinding flare then suddenly winked out. Llew's body jerked. Jade swayed and blinked, a vague look of surprise on her face. Then she collapsed to the ground beside her patient. Brynn ran forward with a cry of fear but Cadoc got there first and lifted her gently in his arms. Llew lay, still and pale, beside them.

Brynn anxiously watched Jade's face then glared at Cadoc. "She's given all her strength to save your friend," he accused.

"I didn't ask her to. She offered," Cadoc said calmly. He glanced over at his friend and reached out to place fingertips on the older man's throat. Then he did the same to Jade.

He shook his head, lay her down on the floor beside her patient and looked regretfully up at Phoenix and Marcus. "I'm sorry. She's dead. They both are."

CHAPTER SIX

Phoenix swore inventively and pushed Cadoc aside to check for himself. He laid his fingers on Jade's slender, white neck and felt for a pulse. Nothing. Next he pulled her dagger out of its sheath and counted the rubies in its hilt twice. Sure enough, of the seven life-rubies with which she had started this game, only five were still sparklingly intact. The other two had dulled and cracked to lifeless chips of pink stone.

He shoved the knife back with a groan and glared at the Player. Cadoc stared back, his grey eyes clouded with regret. He laid a consoling hand on Phoenix's arm. After an internal struggle, Phoenix suppressed his anger enough to speak grudgingly, through gritted teeth.

"It's not your fault. I'm sorry about your friend, too." He stood up and went to stand by the door with his arms folded. "Jade's always giving more than she can; doing more than she should. She's too soft; but at least she has more lives." He ignored Brynns' reproachful glare and Marcus' look of resigned understanding.

Marcus, alone, guessed how hard Phoenix found it to depend on Jade – or anyone.

The group watched for a few heartbeats until the particular 'magic' of this digital world did its job. Colour returned to Jade's pale cheeks. She drew a deep, shuddering breath and began a new life. Her eyes flew open and she stared at the ceiling for a moment before grimacing and sitting up with a moan. Nobody said anything as she pulled out her dagger and looked at the gem-studded hilt. With a sigh, she slid it back into its sheath.

"Thought so," she still sounded tired. "Well, that was unnecessary and stupid, wasn't it? No, don't answer." She held up a hand as Phoenix opened his mouth. "I'm sorry, ok. It's been a long couple of weeks and I just didn't realise how drained I was. It won't happen again, I promise. Oh!"

She twisted around and reached a hand out toward Llew but stopped just before her fingers touched him. Her face crumpled and she knelt beside the man, obviously fighting back tears. Cadoc crouched beside her, draping one arm over her shoulders and pulling her into a sideways hug.

"I'm so sorry," her voice was muffled by her hands. "I tried but his heart stopped and I couldn't get it started again."

"I know," the Player reassured her. "I saw." He peeled the herb poultice back and showed a perfectly-healed shoulder on his friend's body. "You did an incredible job with the healing. I just think he was too old for this adventure. I shouldn't have let him come. I should have chosen a different Companion."

Sighing, he rocked back on his heels and pulled Jade to her feet. "Come on. You and your friends go have breakfast while I make arrangements. Then we'll have to continue our journey."

The four companions edged out of the room, leaving Cadoc to his silent grief. Marcus followed Jade as she stumbled toward the kitchen, saying to Phoenix as he passed, "I'll make sure she eats."

Phoenix nodded gratefully; glad Marcus was there to look after Jade. She was sure to blame herself for this death and Marcus had more patience with her than he did when she was in that sort of mood.

Brynn tugged on his arm, jerking his head to indicate he wanted to speak to him in private. "I don't trust him," he murmured, eyeing the bedroom darkly. "He doesn't even really care that his friend is dead."

Phoenix glanced at the closed door. There was no way to explain to Brynn *why* a Player didn't much care about his digital companion. To Brynn, this was real; to Cadoc, it was just a computer game. Phoenix had mixed feelings about the Player but they had more to do with envy than trust.

"I don't think he's a bad guy, if that's what you mean," he hedged. "It wasn't his fault Jade overdid the healing."

Brynn sent him a knowing, scornful look. "Don't let his pretty face blind you."

Phoenix shook his head. "It's not that. He's fine, Brynn. He's a good fighter and he's got extra lives, like Jade and I do. We need all the help we can get in this world and I'm not going to turn aside someone who knows what's going on just on a whim. We trusted you, remember?"

Brynn glowered at him for a moment then turned away and stalked out the back door.

He disappeared for an hour. When he did return, the confusion of packing, arranging for Llew's burial and taking leave of their kind hosts didn't give Phoenix a chance to talk with him. Overriding Samir's protests, Jade pressed several small, silver Roman coins into Leela's hands as she said goodbye. Phoenix was glad, as the village was too poor to feed and house travellers for free.

The five moved out of the village about mid-morning, heading east along the river. They were followed by twenty or more laughing, skipping, singing brown children and an assortment of scrawny yellow dogs. At the outskirts of the farmland, the children stopped and began waving and calling out good luck messages. Phoenix and Brynn waved back but Jade, deep in conversation with Cadoc, didn't seem to notice. Marcus rode alongside listening, with an expression of polite interest, as Cadoc told stories of some of his adventures. Phoenix and Brynn nudged their horses closer, eavesdropping shamelessly. Together, they rode east, squinting into the rising sun.

"I'm sorry if this sounds rude," Jade said, "but why didn't you want to stay for Llew's funeral?"

Cadoc sent her a surprised look. He waved a hand around at the wide, green world. "I know this is all very realistic but you do remember what he is, don't you? Completing the Quest is more important. You can't afford to let anything get in the way of that."

Jade bit her lip and cast her eyes down. Phoenix guessed she had forgotten that, to Cadoc, this was just a game. Phoenix saw Jade send a speculative, sideways look at Marcus and Brynn. They were supposed to be only digital constructs but it was too easy to forget that. Phoenix wasn't so sure any more. According to the old woman who had come to them in Albion, this world was real in its own way. Everything certainly seemed very real.

Of course, Cadoc was still outside the game, connected only by a virtual headset and a control console. It was weird to think they travelled with someone who didn't really inhabit the body they saw. To him it remained a game; a game he could get out of or switch off any time he wanted to. To him, Llew was nothing more than a construct of that game – not a real person to get emotionally attached to.

Phoenix jumped into the conversation, not wanting Jade to continue a topic that might lead to awkward questions about why she felt so strongly about her Companions.

"So," he called across to the warrior, "what were you doing in the Naga caves?"

Cadoc shrugged. "Got sidetracked by the promise of

treasure. The Naga are famous for being the guardians of huge riches. Unfortunately, they proved to be very *good* guardians. What about you? How did you end up in there?"

"We came into this level through a portal in the Naga caves," he replied diffidently. Behind him, Phoenix could almost feel Brynn's interest and disappointment at the mention of riches lost.

Cadoc's gaze sharpened. "Really? Now that's interesting. We came in through the Karla caves temple in the mountain range toward the west. It's a lot further away, though, so a portal around here would be handy."

Jade shook her head. "The entrance is blocked by a rockfall. Even if you could get past the Naga, you wouldn't be able to get to the gate."

With a sigh, the warrior shrugged. "Oh well."

"Where are you going now?" Jade's expression was easy to read. She felt bad that she'd wrecked his plans. Phoenix sighed. She really was way too trusting. Cadoc seemed like a nice guy but he was still another Player with his own agenda. He was out to win his Game and, if they were in his way, he wouldn't think twice about getting them out of it, one way or another.

Cadoc pointed east. "About twenty-five kilometres downstream the Mula river comes out of these mountain ranges and turns south. There's a small market town there called Punya-Vishaya or Pune. We… Hmmm I'll have to find a new Companion, I suppose." He shook his head as though ridding himself of the memory of his late friend. "Anyway…I need to get to Pune to complete my quest."

"Really? So do we," Jade blurted, apparently forgetting Phoenix's warning. She gasped and slapped a hand over her mouth. Phoenix groaned.

Cadoc laughed, his face lighting up. "Don't worry. It's only if you start talking details about your quest or your real world life that you get in trouble. It's ok to travel together and just chat. I'm glad you're going to Pune."

Jade smiled back. "Me too."

Phoenix closed his eyes and scrubbed a hand over his face. Even *he* could tell she liked Cadoc. How many problems was this going to cause?

As he pondered how to deal with the situation, he saw Jade's expression lighten. She drew a deep breath, sucking in the warm scents of trees and earth. Phoenix followed her gaze as she turned to look around.

It definitely was a heck of a lot nicer than the desert of Egypt. To the north and south, mountain ranges, tiered like giants' steps, rose steeply into the blue sky. Above the farmland valley, tall trees dotted the ridges, changing to deep, lush rainforest in the valleys.

"I smell..." she closed her eyes, "sandalwood, patchouli and lemongrass." She smiled. "It's almost like being at home in my dad's hothouse. I'm so glad to be back amongst the trees."

Cadoc raised his brows and caught Phoenix's eyes in question.

Phoenix shrugged. "We spent a week in the desert on the last level."

"You want trees," Cadoc chuckled, "you should have been with me. I was in South America being chased by spear-waving natives," he pointed to his ruby arm bracelet. "Lost three lives there. One when a spider bit me – how dumb is that?"

Jade laughed. "I could have healed you if I'd been there. In fact, if you happen to see a low-growing plant with kind of thick, hairy leaves, let me know."

"Huh?" He glanced around at the profusion of scrubby plants and new growth in the ploughed fields.

She blushed. "It's Indian Borage – great for coughs, fevers, insect bites and stuff. I use a lot of herbs in my magic."

Phoenix raised his eyes to the sky and shook his head.

Now she was just showing off. He glanced around. Behind, Brynn glowered at Cadoc's back and Marcus' impassive expression had settled into stone.

Cadoc eyed her in obvious admiration. "Really? And do you often have to heal your friends with them?"

"Sure," Jade said with a too-casual shrug. "All the time. In fact, my main job seems to be healing people and coming up with brilliant rescue plans – usually in the other order."

"Well," Cadoc laid a hand on her shoulder, "I'm sure they appreciate all your hard work. I know I would."

Jade fell silent, staring down between her mare's twitching ears. Phoenix watched her, wondering what she was thinking. She flicked him a quick, frowning look, full of doubt and hurt.

The Player murmured something about scouting ahead. He kicked his heels into his mount and trotted away. Jade looked after him for a long moment. Phoenix's sense of unease and annoyance grew. She could have agreed. She could have defended him and the others. Instead, she acted like he was the badguy here.

He edged his stallion closer. Marcus and Brynn came alongside. The four friends rode abreast on the path. Ahead, Cadoc cantered smoothly toward the next bend. Phoenix eyed the man, feeling disgruntled. He rode a magnificent, black war-horse fitted out with the best gear and led Llew's now-empty mount. The Player looked like the perfect warrior – muscular and bristling with pointy weapons. Add to that the fact that he was charming, intelligent and ridiculously good-looking and Cadoc was just so darned perfect it was irritating. He must have scored all twenties when he rolled his character's avatar and skills.

"So what do you think of him?" Phoenix demanded of Marcus.

The Roman watched their fellow traveller for a few

moments, taking his usual amount of time to mull over his answer.

"I'm not sure. There's more to him than there seems," he replied at last. "He is not just a simple sword for hire."

"What do you mean?" Phoenix turned to look at Marcus in surprise. He hadn't actually expected a definitive answer, just an opinion.

"I'm sure I've seen him somewhere before," Marcus admitted. "I just can't remember where. Perhaps Londinium?"

"Yes! That's it!" Brynn slapped his thigh. "I thought the same thing. Now I remember. I stabled his horse for him when he came through our village just a few days before I met you two. He and his father were riding to Londinium to meet the Roman Governor. He paid me a measly copper piece – cheapskate."

"He went to see my father, Agricola?" Marcus asked. Brynn nodded and Marcus narrowed his eyes thoughtfully. "Yes. You're right. Now I remember. His father is Corio, King of the Dobunnic territories. They came to make a deal with my father. Corio retained his title and territory in return for tithing half his peoples' crops to Rome. He also, if I remember correctly, met with Zhudai in private. Cadoc did not attend the meetings, though."

"Half!" Brynn was appalled. "How could they survive?"

"I don't think King Corio cared." Marcus' grim expression said everything.

"But you can't blame Cadoc for his father's greed," Jade interrupted. "Maybe he even left the country to get away from what his father was doing – like you did, Marcus. Don't judge him on his father. You said he wasn't in the meetings. Anyway, *I* like him."

Marcus bowed his head but his eyes were hard. "You're right, of course."

"So he's a Prince, is he?" Phoenix regretted the

comment immediately.

Jade's green eyes took on a dreamy expression while Marcus' frown deepened and Brynn began to glower again.

"I still say he's a cheapskate," the boy muttered, glaring at Jade.

Jade huffed and urged her mare into a trot so she could catch up with her new friend. Phoenix exchanged worried looks with Marcus but there was really nothing they could do, so they went to join her.

Cadoc's charismatic charm rapidly overcame the moment of awkwardness that followed and the group soon laughed and chatted as they rode through the sultry morning. The green, terraced mountains that wrapped around the river gradually opened up and the floodplain widened. They passed a village that lay on the north side of the Mula river but its people didn't seem as friendly as those of Paud. Brightly-clad women, casting the travellers scared, hurried looks, ushered their children inside. Barechested men working in the fields, stopped to stare silently as they passed; dark eyes narrowed and knuckles white on their tools.

Phoenix glanced across at Jade, wondering what she made of it. It didn't look like she'd even noticed. She was busy talking with Cadoc. Under his attention, she blossomed: laughing and smiling, flirting even. In fact, he'd never seen her so relaxed and happy.

He had to admit, it was hard to dislike Cadoc. He laughed openly and frequently, white teeth flashing and eyes crinkling in genuine amusement. Phoenix sighed, trying to keep perspective. He seemed a nice enough guy and if he could keep Jade in good spirits after the morning's disaster then Phoenix was willing to try and put aside his own childish jealousy and automatic distrust and get along with him.

By early afternoon the sun beat down on their bare heads. They were all hungry and sweaty. Having forded a small river that joined the Mula, they now approached a smaller series of mountain ridges.   According to Cadoc, once they rounded this last arm of the mountain range, the Mula would turn southeast and lead them straight to Pune before nightfall. As they headed for the shade of a large fig tree to eat lunch and water the horses, Phoenix reflected on what had been a surprisingly calm morning.

The group dismounted. Phoenix heard Cadoc growl and Jade sigh. Behind him, Brynn groaned.

"Oh, come *on*. We only just *got* here. Don't we even get time to eat now?"

Phoenix looked around and froze.

Stepping out from behind the huge tree and standing in a loose semi-circle, were thirty or more men. They all bore weapons and basic uniforms of a white shirt and a once-white dhoti; but all of them looked worse-for-wear.

In fact, they looked like they could use a good feed. Gold-brown skin stretched tightly over delicate bones and stomachs that were clearly empty. Their clothing hung in tatters and their weapons were notched and rusted. Feet, calloused from lack of shoes, carried thin bodies topped by gaunt faces and lank, black hair. Only their dark eyes seemed alive – sparkling with hunger, desperation and a hint of fear. One of them stepped forward half a pace, raising a ragged-edged, curved sword.

"Give us everything and we will spare your lives," he snarled, showing broken, yellowed teeth.

Jade stepped forward and pushed back a piece of white linen she'd draped over her head to protect her face from the sun. "You poor things. You look half-starved. Let me-"

"*Vetaala!*" the leader gasped, pointing.

His eyes widened and his hand shook. He took a wobbly step back, almost colliding with one of his fellows. The others took up the word; whispering it at first then crying it aloud when Jade held out a hand toward them.

"No, no!" she denied. "Please, I'm not."

It was too late. At the sound of her voice, the pack broke. Staggering and screaming, the would-be robbers turned and fled down the long valley. In silent amazement, the companions watched until the last of them vanished into the scrubby forest and their high-pitched yells had faded. High overhead, a circling eagle cried in imitation.

CHAPTER SEVEN

As one, Phoenix, Marcus and Brynn looked blankly at each other and then at Jade.

"Well," Phoenix laughed, "I hope all our fights are that easy."

Jade drew up her head-cloth again, hiding the white-blonde hair, green eyes and pale skin that had caused such a ruckus.

"*What* was it they called you?" He grinned at her discomfiture.

"I don't know," she said tartly. "They were so starved they were probably hallucinating anyway."

"No," he replied, unable to resist teasing her, "I'm pretty sure I heard them call you a ghost."

"Vampire," Brynn put in, giggling. "It was definitely their word for vampire."

"Oh shut up." Jade turned to her horse and made a show of loosening the saddle-girth.

"A vampire," Brynn repeated faintly, still laughing. Phoenix couldn't help chuckling along with him. It was pretty funny.

Ignoring them, Jade tied up her mare and started pulling out supplies with more force than was strictly needed. Phoenix looked at her, feeling a twinge of guilt as he spotted a sheen of tears in her eyes. She dashed them away.

Cadoc went over and tied his mount alongside her

mare. She turned her face away. Phoenix edged forward, trying to hear their low conversation. He glared as Cadoc rested a sympathetic hand on hers.

"I'm sure they don't mean to hurt you," the Player said simply.

She shrugged one shoulder. "I know. I'm just…tired."

"We all are but that's no excuse. A leader should…" He stopped, closing his lips with a sidelong glance at Phoenix.

She sighed.

Phoenix felt the sharp sting of anger when, again, she didn't defend him. He scowled at her. He was *trying* to be a leader but he wasn't perfect. She wasn't perfect either. Sometimes he couldn't help acting his real age. Not even Marcus and Brynn knew that Jade and Phoenix were both not even fourteen years old in the real world. Couldn't a guy have any fun here anymore? He laid a hand on Blódbál's hilt and the anger flared higher. Startled, he took his hand off and backed away, shaken by the strength of his own reaction.

Cadoc put his hands on Jade's shoulders, turned her toward the tree and gave her a little push.

"Why don't you let me get the lunch? You look like you could use a rest."

"Th..thanks," she stuttered, staring at him.

Phoenix's anger faded into guilt as he watched her smile gratefully at the Player. He grimaced. Clearly he'd overstepped the mark and really hurt her feelings. Another quick look at Marcus told him everything he needed to know. Marcus was like a weather-vane for the group morale. If Phoenix did the wrong thing, all he had to do was look at Marcus' normally-calm expression. A slight frown on that handsome face meant he'd been more than usually stupid. So that dark scowl meant he'd really stuffed up this time.

OK, the whole vampire thing had been a bit juvenile but the expressions on those Indian guys' faces had been priceless. Phoenix sighed and scrubbed a hand through his hair. Being an adult; being a leader – it was all a lot harder than he'd ever thought it would be.

Cadoc's presence wasn't making that job any easier, either. Phoenix felt intimidated and unsettled with the handsome Player in the group. His presence subtly affected their relationships. Now, more than ever, their group had to work together. Phoenix couldn't afford to alienate Jade or be angry at any of his friends again. Resting his hand on the hilt of Blódbál reminded him of that. The sword sang its unsubtle spell-song in his head, urging him to fight, kill and die. He had to resist it or it would control him through his already-quick temper.

He walked over and laid a hand on Jade's shoulder. She sent him a hurt, flickering look.

"Sorry." He cleared his throat, feeling awkward. "That was stupid. I'm an idiot."

She looked at him expressionlessly for a moment then pressed her lips together and nodded. "Yeah, you are sometimes but so am I." She sighed. "I guess I was feeling guilty about losing another life, losing Llew and letting Cadoc down...so I kinda overreacted when you teased me. Plus," she pressed her fingers to her pale, heat-flushed cheeks, "I'm not feeling one hundred percent."

"What's wrong?" Not really knowing how to deal with her confused emotions, Phoenix wrapped loving fingers around the hilt of his sword, glancing around in the hopes of seeing a more physical danger he could just chop up instead.

"No, it's just..." she hesitated then shook her head. "No, nothing really. Just feeling a bit off. I'll be ok. Thanks, though."

Relieved, he gave her a thumbs-up and went off to answer a call of nature.

After lunch, they packed their gear in more comfortable silence, mounted and continued to ride, following the river downstream. The humid heat was more draining than the dry heat of Egypt and they were all drooping by the time they neared the last of the foothills.

Jade called a halt and sat on her mare, staring into the dusty northeastern horizon.

"What is it?" Phoenix edged his horse alongside hers, shoving in between her and Cadoc.

"I thought I saw a flash of something metal out on the plains." She shaded her eyes. Everyone watched but her Elven eyesight far outstripped theirs.

All he saw was a great pall of dust hanging over the flatlands. Eventually, she shook her head and shrugged.

They rode on for a few minutes then Marcus spoke up. "Did anyone else notice that those men all wore a uniform of some sort?"

The group halted, staring at each other in consternation. As one, they turned to look again at the dustcloud ahead.

"You don't think…" Brynn began.

"Yes," Marcus said. "I think there's probably a very large army somewhere under that cloud of dust."

"I'd say you're right." Cadoc frowned and nodded toward the nearby ridge. "Perhaps we should head up to higher ground and get a look ahead before we run straight into a full-blown war."

Phoenix gritted his teeth, annoyed he hadn't thought of it. Everyone else took it for granted that Cadoc's idea was a good one and turned their mounts to follow his. Reluctantly, Phoenix did the same. It *was* a good idea, after all.

It took them longer than expected to find a safe path up to the top of the ridge. Underfoot, broken blocks of black basalt made riding and walking equally hazardous. It was hard to look where they put their feet and watch for ambushes at the same time.

By the time they finally reached the summit, the sun balanced on jagged mountaintops behind them. Overhead, streaky clouds once more flamed with the hot pinks and oranges of a subtropical sunset. Shadows lengthened. Night was not far away and they had not yet reached Pune.

They peered through the gathering dusk. Spread out below, a vast floodplain stretched to the eastern horizon and beyond. To the west, the massive mountain range from which they had come marched unbroken to the north and south as far as they could see. Slowly, the sun sank behind the western peaks and their jagged shadows speared across the plain. The sky darkened to purple and the first stars began to come out. Below, as though the sky had fallen to earth, dozens of little sparks of light flickered to life on the dark floodplain. Flickering like earth-stars, more and more popped into existence as the friends watched in awe.

"There are…thousands and thousands of them," Brynn whispered.

"Campfires," Marcus said. "If we assume there're maybe ten men around each fire, there must be over-"

"A hundred thousand," Cadoc finished.

Phoenix frowned at him. "You sound pretty certain. How do you know for sure?"

The warrior shrugged. "Llew and I heard about it as we travelled this way from Karla Caves. Bhumaka, a king of sorts from the coast - over those western mountains - was coming behind us from his base in Śūrpāraka, with an army of a hundred thousand men. He's trying to stop some petty king on this side of the mountains from getting too big for his boots. I was hoping to get to Pune before their armies destroyed it. Knew I shouldn't have bothered with the Naga treasure."

"Well thanks for sharing," Phoenix said sarcastically.

Cadoc spread his hands. "Like I said, I thought we'd get to Pune first. The army moved faster than I anticipated."

"So where is Pune from here?" Jade jumped in.

He pointed just south of east, into the inky night. "It will be about ten kilometres that way. You can't see anything because there are still a couple of hills in the way. It's only small, anyway."

"Can we just cut straight across to it and bypass the army completely?" Brynn suggested.

"Hang on, I'll check." Cadoc stood still and stared blankly off into space for several moments.

Phoenix exchanged knowing looks with Jade. Cadoc was probably Googling Pune on a map – looking for the best route to the town. It was kind of eerie to have their new companion put himself on pause.

Seconds later, he blinked and they knew he'd returned to the game. "There are two valleys and two more high ridges between us and the town. If we try and climb them at night, we'll break an ankle. If we do it during the day, we're sure to be spotted by the army scouts and captured as spies."

"Fabulous," Phoenix grumbled. "So what, we're stuck up here until the army moves on?"

Cadoc shook his head. "They're not going to move on in a hurry, I'm afraid. Llew and I heard that the other army is coming in from the northeast. Bhumaka will most likely take possession of Pune then ford the river and meet the other army on the plains north of the city. They may even raze the town to the ground – which would make completing our Quests pretty difficult, I'd say."

Phoenix began to pace, sending irritated glances at the twinkling army camp below.

"Would we be able to negotiate safe passage into Pune to complete our quest without getting involved in the war?" Marcus asked.

The Player shrugged. "I don't know but once you walk into the middle of an army and offer money, what's to stop them from killing you and taking it anyway?"

"A point," Marcus conceded.

"I could just sneak in to Pune and complete the Quest myself," Brynn offered."

"I don't *think* so," Jade replied witheringly.

"But I *could*," he insisted.

"And what would we do, sit here and wait?" she said. "As if. I'm not letting you get killed again." She gripped the boy's shoulder and squeezed hard until he squeaked in protest. Cadoc sent her a quizzical look, which she ignored.

Phoenix sighed, shelving his instinctive desire for action with difficulty. They needed to think this through first. "I don't know about you lot but I'm tired and hungry. Why don't we camp for the night and see how it looks in the morning?"

"Sounds good to me." Cadoc jerked a thumb over his shoulder. "I saw a spring in a thicket of trees just back there. Should be enough fodder for the horses as well as water and shelter."

Phoenix suppressed another irrational surge of envy. *He* should have been to the one to spot a camping place. He shook his head at his own reaction. He had to stop comparing himself to Cadoc. It was not helpful.

Jade sent some witchlights to hover low over the broken ground ahead as they made their way slowly and carefully back to the spring. Cadoc was right: it was a perfect campsite. Their fire was sheltered and hidden by a thick grove of trees surrounding a crystal clear natural spring that bubbled out of the mountainside. Nearby, a small, grassy clearing provided food for the horses. Once Jade created the illusion of a fence between the trees, the horses seemed quite content to stay there.

They were a merry enough group. Dinner was a thick stew made of bits and pieces from both lots of supplies and supplemented with some of the flatbreads the Indian villagers ate. Leela had given Jade the breads and a bag of spices for seasoning when they'd left that morning. Jade added some of the spices to the pot; Cadoc threw in a few dried vegetables and Brynn added a freshly-dressed hare he had brought down with a casual shot from his sling. Along with a skin of wine from Heron's stock, it was a delicious, filling meal.

Afterward, they reclined in various states of half-sleep, gazing at the small fire in comfortable silence. Brynn brought out the little bronze whistle given to him in Svealand and piped a quiet, drowsy little tune. The flames flickered and danced hypnotically, occasionally sending tiny sparks sailing into a dark sky. The smell of woodsmoke reminded Phoenix of camping trips in Scotland with his parents but not even the thought of his father could bother him at the moment.

He sat now with his back against a tree, eyelids drooping, content and relaxed. For once, no-one was chasing them, imprisoning them or attempting to kill them. It was a welcome relief. This was what adventures should be like. So much for Level Four being harder than Level three. Apart from a small brush with a large number of snake-people and Jade being careless with a life, it was all going pretty easily. They just had to bypass an inconvenient army and they'd be home free. They were sure to come up with a good plan for that after a decent night's sleep.

Idly, Phoenix considered sliding off into sleep right where he was but his neck was already stiff and a rock was dug into his backside. Besides, if he put up his leather tent, he'd be protected from the dew. At least then he'd get a few hours sleep before his watch.

Yawning, he shook his head. His thinking was getting a little muzzy but it did occur to him that no-one had even talked about setting watch. Jade was usually almost compulsive about it. Uneasy, he glanced around at his friends and frowned. They had all actually dropped off to sleep. Cadoc lay buried under a pile of blankets on the other side of the fire. Brynn had fallen on to his side and now snored loudly, his head pillowed on Jade's backpack. Jade was curled up under her cloak, her beautiful face relaxed and unworried for a change. Even Marcus slept soundly, his sword still lying in his open hand.

Phoenix sighed. It seemed like the first watch belonged to him. Well, he'd better add wood to the fire and find somewhere a little less comfortable to sit; otherwise he'd be snoozing, too.

He reached out a hand to push himself off the ground. It wouldn't move. He stared at his arm in confusion. OK, the other one, then. That one refused to move, either. What was wrong with him? With a huge effort, he raised his heavy head and looked blearily around the campsite. Was that a flicker of movement in the trees?

Fear gave his body a shot of adrenalin. His right hand crept across his lap towards Blódbál's hilt. If he could just get hold of the sword, its magic would wake him up.

Before he could reach it, fifty or more men stepped into the firelight, their dark eyes and sharp swords glittering. The last thing Phoenix remembered was the point of a blade pricking at his throat. Then darkness claimed his mind.

CHAPTER EIGHT

Jade awoke with a splitting headache and a mouth tasting of mouldy cotton wool. Screwing up her face, she cracked one eye open and immediately regretted it. Daylight stabbed her eyeball, exploded into her brain and sent chills of nausea flooding through her body. Was this what a hangover felt like? If so, then when she got back to the real world, she would never, ever get drunk.

She desperately needed some water to clear her mouth. Then she'd be able to at least say a healing spell that would clear the headache and nausea. She dry-swallowed down the queasiness. Next she tried to roll over and made an unpleasant discovery: her hands were tied tightly behind her back.

What? Who?

Suddenly the headache didn't seem so important. Lying still, Jade sifted through her memories of the night before. They had made camp, made dinner, eaten it, …and then what? All she remembered was watching the fire and feeling more and more drowsy. Surely they hadn't all fallen asleep without setting watch? How could they?

A sudden flash of recall made her want to groan. The spices. She had put those spices from Leela into their stew. The Indian woman must have drugged them. But why?

To find that out, she'd have to open her eyes again. Under her breath, she muttered the healing spell. It wasn't one hundred percent effective but at least it took the edge off the headache. Cautiously, she opened an eye and found the dim daylight bearable. She seemed to be lying on dirt, on her side in some sort of large tent. There were other lumpy shapes around her. One of them moved and groaned. It sounded like Brynn.

She wriggled over to him and put her mouth near his ear. "Brynn…wake up."

The boy's body jerked. His eyes flew open then screwed shut again. He opened his mouth then clamped it shut when Jade spoke.

She whispered. "Don't throw up and don't make any noise! We're tied up in a tent somewhere. I think we were drugged last night. Stay still a moment."

Brynn was silent for a few seconds, his eyes firmly closed, his throat working as he held down the nausea. Finally he gave her a tight grin through clenched teeth.

"Number six, huh? Well, at least no-one's killed me yet." He grimaced. "Although I almost wish they had."

With a grunt of effort, Jade twisted and squirmed until she managed to pull her feet through her looped arms and brought her hands up in front of her. Touching Brynn's head, she murmured the healing spell again and heard him sigh in relief.

"I need to help the others," she whispered in his ear. "You work on getting yourself free."

Brynn nodded and repeated her trick of getting his hands to the front. It paid to be flexible. Casting frequent, wary glances at the tent-flap, Jade struggled over to Phoenix. One by one, she applied the healing spell on him, Marcus and Cadoc; whispering instructions and reassurance as they came awake. Unfortunately, none of them could get their feet through their hands – they were less flexible and just too well-tied. The knots were too tight for her or Brynn to work loose.

Worried, Jade whispered *harken* and closed her eyes. Blocking out the small noises her friends made, she listened beyond the tent walls, trying to find out how much time they might have before someone arrived to check on them. It was impossible. There were so many conversations going on and so many other, weird noises that there was no way she could pick out what might refer to herself. She heard fires crackling, horses stamping, laughter and drowsy complaints; harsh orders and whispered insubordination. Then, from somewhere close by, came a bizarre trumpeting that almost blasted her sensitised eardrums.

Pulling her mind back into her skull, Jade groaned. The headache returned with a vengeance and a repeat of the healing spell barely scratched it this time. She needed her herbs and some water.

"What was *that?*" Brynn squeaked, awed by the noise.

"An elephant." Marcus sounded grim. "I've seen them in the Games in Rome and my father sometimes uses them in battle. We must be in the army camp."

"It sounds huge!" Brynn looked apprehensively up at the tent roof.

"They are," Marcus agreed. "But what are they doing here? I thought they came from Africa."

"There're are some in India, too," Cadoc said in a low tone. "Indian kings put armour on them and use them in battle here, too. In an army this size, there will probably be at least a thousand elephants as well as horse cavalry."

"Who cares," Phoenix whispered. "I just want to know how we get out of here – with all our stuff. They've taken my sword."

Jade gasped and patted awkwardly at the front of her shirt with her fingers. She slumped in relief. The Hyllion Bagia was still there, under her shirt, tucked into her waistband. Her dagger and staff were gone, along with her backpack but their captors hadn't found the Bag or her amulet.

She caught Phoenix's eye, about to reassure him but he shook his head at her. Startled, she raised an eyebrow. He glanced at Cadoc and shook his head firmly again. The message was clear. For some reason, Phoenix didn't want the Player to know about the Bag.

Annoyed, Jade pressed her lips together and frowned at him. She supposed it made sense but it felt wrong to withhold such vital information from their fellow captive. He was as much a victim as they were. Along with their Quest-item, the Sudarsharna, the Bag contained all sorts of useful items: torches, food, Roman weapons and money. For a long moment, Jade debated ignoring Phoenix's warning and revealing the Bag anyway. Just as she had almost decided to do so, her Elven ears heard approaching footsteps.

"Down!" she hissed and flopped down on her side, facing away from the tent opening. Once more she extended her hearing, focussing on the approaching soldiers. This time she got luckier.

"I'd rather Lord Bhumaka sent someone else to bring the prisoners to his tent," one of the soldiers muttered.

"You scared of Bhumaka?" the other jeered.

"No – well, yes but not this time. I'm more worried about the prisoners," the first said hurriedly. "Haven't you heard? One of them is a…vetaala."

"A vampire?" his friend scoffed. "I heard the rumour when the scout group came back yesterday but I don't believe it. They're not real."

"Oh? And I suppose you don't believe in the Naga, either?"

"Them, I believe in," the second man said, fear in his voice. "I just can't believe Lord Bhumaka has made an alliance with them. You can't trust the snake-people. It gives me the creeps just to see them in our camp. Is it true that they are going to fight on our side against Guatamiputra Satakarni?"

"I don't know and I don't want to know," the first man replied. "I just want to get this job done and get away from all of this. I'm a merchant. I'm of the vaishya caste, not a soldier. I've got a dozen fishermen to manage back in Śūrpāraka. We should leave soldiering to the Kshatriya caste. I don't even see why we're fighting for the Saka, anyway. Everyone knows that Guatamiputra is the real Raj, not Bhumaka."

"Hush!" his companion hissed. "Don't say that near one of the Saka troops if you value your life. The pay is good, that's all you have to worry about. Who cares who calls themselves Raj, as long as there's enough food to feed our families?"

Jade had heard more than enough. Her heart raced. If the Naga were in league with this Bhumaka then the last thing she and her friends needed was to be hauled into his tent. The Naga would be sure to recognise their attackers and demand vengeance. She didn't understand everything the men said about castes and Sakas but one thing was clear – somehow they had to escape or change their faces before being taken before Bhumaka and his Naga allies.

That was it! She held her breath as a kernel of an idea flickered in her head. Rolling over, she jerked her head at the others.

"Here they come. Pretend to be more ill than you are and whatever you do, don't look surprised when you see each other. Cadoc, you're a mute. Don't speak."

Understandably, they sent her confused, blank looks but she didn't have time to explain. Instead, she closed her eyes and drew on as much power as she dared. Her own appearance had to be first as she was the most remarkable of the group. She drew a mental picture of Leela's oldest daughter, Mallika. Superimposing Mallika's pretty, brown-skinned image over her own face in her mind, Jade whispered the Elvish illusion spell and heard Brynn gasp in amazement.

There was no time for talk. The soldiers were almost at the door. The footsteps came closer, slower now as the men's reluctance to see a vampire dragged at their feet. Jade concentrated on each of the others in turn, replacing their faces with illusions of men and a boy from the village. It wasn't easy. She hadn't really taken much notice of individual faces. Hopefully the change would be just enough to make Bhumaka believe he was dealing with a group of natives, rather than outlanders. Their clothes and gear could be a problem. She didn't have enough strength to change everything and her powers wouldn't work on anything iron, anyway. Hopefully the others would catch on and someone would come up with a plausible story to explain their gear.

It was done just as the soldiers shoved back the tent flap and barked a harsh order.

"Get up. Lord Bhumaka has commanded your presence."

With more groaning than was strictly necessary, the friends struggled to their feet. Jade cast another surreptitious look at her companions. If it wasn't for their clothes, she wouldn't have recognised any of them. Brynn looked much like himself but with darker skin and hair. Marcus and Cadoc were similarly altered. She just hoped she could maintain it. She didn't like their chances as obvious outlanders in the middle of an army. Now they just had to come up with a good reason why a bunch of Indian natives were dressed as foreigners.

As they marched at spearpoint through the camp, she could almost feel Marcus' disapproval. He had grown up in Roman army camps. Discipline and organisation were the keys to a Roman army. Most of the men were full-time soldiers: living and breathing the army life; bonded in eight-man tent-groups; marching all over Europe; seasoned fighters.

This camp was definitely not Roman. It seemed to be made up of motley groups, scattered in disorderly fashion over the field. Most were Indian men but there were some women and even a few children scurrying about. Clearly, the men were not regular soldiers. Uniforms were sketchy and tattered at best; most men didn't have tents or bedding of any sort; food seemed scarce and cooking utensils minimal; skinny dogs roamed wild, snapping at anyone who approached; weapons were dull and notched. The only things that seemed well cared-for were the elephants.

Jade watched with amusement as Brynn's expression changed to slack-jawed wonder as they passed near to an elephant-handler's area. Five enormous beasts were tethered with nothing more than a thin piece of rope tied to a small metal stake in the ground. Piled on the ground nearby were random stacks of plate armour and bales of hay. As the group passed, one of the large males raised his trunk, pointed his long white tusks to the sky and trumpeted loudly. The rest of the elephants shuffled restlessly and rubbed their trunks across each others' grey, wrinkled backs as if seeking reassurance.

Jade could have used some reassurance herself. Her illusion gave them at least half a chance of getting out of this alive but it would take more than her minor, and at the moment quite weak, magic to regain their freedom. Somehow, they had to get their gear back *and* escape from the middle of a one-hundred-thousand strong army.

As they moved further through the camp, she noticed a change in the atmosphere. In this area, about a third of the army were clearly not native Indians. Better organised into close-knit groups, these soldierly factions became more common as the companions marched through the camp toward their destination.

The soldiers had paler skin than the Indians. Instead of the dhoti, they wore long coats, decorated trousers, short boots and odd, pointed hats that made them look like overgrown garden gnomes. Scary garden gnomes with fierce expressions, long, dark hair and full beards. Many were practicing archery; using recurve bows with deadly skill.   Some were mock-fighting with battle-axes and knives. Big gnomes you didn't want to mess with.

Realising who they must be from the guard's conversation, Jade leaned over and whispered 'Saka' into Marcus' ear. He frowned and nodded. Then she said the word into Phoenix's ear but whatever Marcus knew, Phoenix didn't.   He just gave her a look of non-comprehension and shrugged. She wasn't much wiser. Whoever these Saka were, wherever they came from, they seemed to make up the fighting core of an otherwise rag-tag army of Indian recruits.

Their Indian guards shoved them toward a large pavilion in the middle of the army. A huge, round tent made of gaudy silks and fluttering flags, it had to be the residence of someone important. At the entrance stood two, expressionless Saka. Gleaming spears were angled across the doorway.

The steps of their escort soldiers faltered as the group approached the tent. Apparently common footsoldiers were wary of the elite troops that guarded their leader. They stopped about fifteen feet away from the door and stood, shuffling their feet. One of them prodded Phoenix in the back with the butt of his spear.

"Go on then. Lord Bhumaka is waiting for you," he grunted.

Jade glanced at Phoenix and shrugged. It wasn't like they had many options. There was little chance of escape from the middle of a one-hundred-thousand strong army. Phoenix nodded back. He drew a deep breath, he pulled back his shoulders. By the way his bound fingers clenched and opened and he frowned down at his left hip, Jade guessed he missed Blódbál. She had to admit, as much as she found his berserker link to that sword frightening, it was also reassuring to know they had a magic sword on their side. Without it, how could they succeed?

Marcus nudged her and jerked his chin toward one side

of the tent. She saw and frowned. Phoenix saw and grinned. Clearly he thought the odds in their favour had just increased. Jade wasn't so sure.

CHAPTER NINE

Stepping between the two rigid guards, the companions filed into the tent and blinked at the opulence inside. Phoenix suppressed a shiver and a sense of deja vu, remembering a similar situation back in England when they'd confronted Agricola, the Roman Governor.

He'd thought Agricola's pavilion luxurious but it was nothing compared to this one. The place was hung with floaty, transparent drapes of silk in vibrant reds, golds, purples and blues; gold-braided ribbons tied them back. More gold braid dangled from dozens of large, bright cushions that lay, scattered around the room. Four huge, decorative rugs in clashing colours and overlapped on the floor. Incense wafted up in smoky spirals from a brass bowl in the centre of the room, its scent sickening. The day was warm, making the inside of the pavilion stuffy and hot.

A man reclined regally on several of the cushions. As they entered, he glanced at them from under heavy lids and smiled. He rose to his feet and the group moved back a pace. He was tall and intimidating with long thick, grey-streaked hair and beard, piercing dark eyes and a hawk nose. His clothing represented an odd combination of richly embroidered Indian silks made into trousers and a coat of the style worn by the Saka soldiers outside. It looked like he wanted to embrace all things Indian but couldn't quite leave his own culture behind.

Walking around them, he eyed his five prisoners. He

clapped his hands and waited, still staring at them. A slender, sari-clad Indian woman arrived and bowed low. Thin gold chains dangled from her hair, earrings and nose ring, gleaming in the sunlight that filtered softly through the pavilion walls. The man murmured something inaudible in her ear and she bowed again, leaving them.

Now their host smiled and inclined his head. "I am Bhumaka, *Kshatrapa* of Ariaca."

No-one spoke. Phoenix said nothing for fear of displaying his ignorance. If he was supposed to be a native, he should know what the heck a Kshatrapa was and where Ariaca was. Their host, however, didn't seem bothered by the silence.

The Indian woman returned with several others, bearing a low, round table. They set it down on the exotic floor-rugs and placed cushions around it. Next they scurried silently in and out of the tent, bringing dish after dish of delicious-smelling foods. When the table groaned under the weight of food, the servants slipped away, leaving the companions to exchange uneasy glances.

Brynn's stomach rumbled loudly.

Were they to be drugged again or treated as honoured guests? Did they eat or not?

Bhumaka caught sight of their faces and smiled. He clapped his hands and his serving woman reappeared, bowed at his gentle request and vanished again. She returned leading a small child by the hand. The boy, about seven years old, blinked solemn dark eyes up at Bhumaka and bowed. He was dressed as a miniature Saka warrior, with trousers, boots, long coat and pointed hat. He even had a jewelled belt dagger and a small bow slung across his back. Bhumaka waved him forward and the woman left again. The boy sat at the table, laying his bow to one side. Bhumaka sat also. At a nod, they both began to pile chapatti, vegetables and meats onto wooden plates before them.

The Kshatrapa of Ariaca gestured at his guests. "Come. Eat. This is my son, Nahapana. As you see, he eats, too."

Brynn edged toward the table, eyeing the food.

"My lord," Marcus spoke first, "is it customary to make guests eat with their hands tied?"

Phoenix held his breath. It was a key point. Were they guests or were they prisoners?

Bhumaka paused, raising a thin brow at the Roman. Then he smiled slightly.

"I admire your boldness, young man. You are right. Where are my manners?" He got to his feet and drew his dagger, slicing the ropes binding their hands.

Phoenix rubbed his wrists, feeling his fingers tingle as blood returned. Now if he could just bargain his gear and sword back, he'd feel a whole lot better about their situation. There was something not quite right about this. Why was Bhumaka being so…nice?

He eased himself down onto the cushions. Instead of sitting cross-legged, he sat in *seiza* – the kneeling position used in his aikido dojo back home. It was hard to get up fast from a cross-legged position but he could move quickly on his knees. He ate sparingly from several exotic dishes in the hopes it would ease his hunger without allowing too much of a drug into his system, if there was one.

"I'm hoping you can…help me." Bhumaka waved a rolled-up flat bread in their direction. "I'm looking for a group of outlanders. Two men, a woman and a boy." He cast them a swift, assessing look from beneath his eyelashes. "The woman, it is said, so pale as to be almost ghostly."

From the corner of his eye, Phoenix saw Jade stiffen.

"No, my lord," he jumped in to prevent her expressive face from revealing too much. "We haven't seen any such in our travels. What have these outlanders done?"

"Oh," Bhumaka shrugged, "I simply represent certain parties who are interested in their whereabouts. But since you haven't seen them, it is of no matter. Please, eat."

There was a small, uncomfortable silence as Phoenix and his friends turned that over in their heads. There was only one party they could think of who might even have any idea of where they were in this world – Feng Zhudai.

The goddess, Anuket had banished Zhudai back to China, so he couldn't interfere directly with their quest in India. She had warned them that their arch-enemy still had far-reaching influences and would continue to try and stop them at every turn. If Bhumaka reported to Zhudai then they needed to get out of here, and fast.

"So, in your…travels… where have you come from?" the Kshatrapa asked.

Phoenix's brain was a little fuzzy. The question took him by surprise. Blinking, he shook it and took a deep breath. The sickly scent of incense caught in his throat and he coughed, stalling for time before answering. He had no idea where they were, in relation to the rest of India – or even the rest of the world. He'd never been very good at geography.

"Um…the south?" he hedged.

Luckily, Bhumaka didn't seem inclined to press for details. Instead, he asked their names. Once more Phoenix was stumped. Put on the spot, he couldn't remember enough Indian names to substitute for their own. Jade came to his rescue.

"I am Jaya, my lord," she said then pointed to Brynn, Marcus, Cadoc and himself in turn. "This is Bala, Marut, Chandak, who is mute, and Pran, my brother."

Bhumaka turned amazed eyes on Phoenix. "You let a woman speak for you?"

"Er…" he shrugged, ignoring her indignant gasp. "Sometimes I find it's best, my lord."

Their host smiled. "You are wise. In Saka society,

women sometimes even fight alongside men but the Indian culture is lamentably unbalanced. Women are often little more than property or slaves. So it is not just your clothing that is unusual for an Indian, Pran."

"Ah," Phoenix plucked at his shirt, "yes… our clothes. I can explain, actually."

Bhumaka held up a hand. "There is no need. I wouldn't put you to the trouble. Besides, I have some friends I'd like you to meet." He rose and bowed to them. "Nahapana will entertain you while I go greet my other guests. We will return momentarily. Excuse me."

After he left, the group sat in silence for a few seconds, ignoring the young Saka prince. Cadoc slid closer to Phoenix, his eyes on the exit.

"What was that all about? Who's this kid? Who was that guy and where's he gone?" He spoke in the only language he could: ancient Breton. Not having the advantage of the magical ability to understand and speak all languages, he'd missed the whole conversation and was obviously annoyed.

Explaining the situation quickly, Phoenix replied in the same language, so the boy wouldn't understand, either. Cadoc's frown deepened with each sentence.

"Bhumaka is looking for you lot, specifically? But not me? That doesn't make sense. His scouting group yesterday saw five of us, not four; and when they brought us in last night, Jade hadn't cast her illusion so they would have seen her real face." Cadoc's expression became grim. "He's just playing games with us. He knows exactly who you are. He just wants you to be offguard when this guest of his arrives. Who could it be, I wonder?"

Jade gasped, her hand covering her mouth. Leaning over, she waved the others closer. "I didn't have time to tell you before. I listened in on the soldiers who came to get us. Bhumaka has made an allegiance with the Naga. They are going to fight on his side against the true king of this area, Guatamiputra Satakarni."

Cadoc swore. "If it's one of them Bhumaka is bringing back to meet us, we are *major* trouble. We will not be popular after that stunt in the mountain. We have to get out of here."

"But there's no way we can make it," Brynn hissed. "We have no weapons and all of our gear has been taken."

Phoenix grinned at Marcus, who frowned back. "If anyone can think of a way to get us safely out of this tent, Marcus spotted our horses and gear all nicely waiting for us just outside."

"I saw them," Jade frowned and shook her head, "but it makes no sense. Why would they do that? Why would they leave our stuff conveniently lying about for us to take? That's stupid."

Phoenix shrugged. "Don't look a gift horse in the mouth. They're dumb, that's all. We get out, you cast a few spells to clear the way, we hack a path out of here and we're gone. Ideas?" He glanced around the others, ignoring her worried expression.

Cadoc grinned wickedly. "I have the perfect plan. Just leave it to me and play along. Not only will it get us out of the tent, it will ensure safe passage out of the whole camp."

"I like the sound of that," Phoenix said, thumping their new friend on the shoulder.

Jade held up a finger. "Whatever you're going to do, make it fast. I hear them coming back."

Moments later, the rear tent flap was pushed aside and Bhumaka entered, smiling. Behind him came a tall well-built Indian, unarmed and wearing plain, dark clothes. The lower half of his face was covered by a strip of dark cloth. He moved with the smooth efficiency of a killer. Phoenix marked him immediately as one to watch out for.

After him came a Naga, slithering on his thick, mottled snake-body; human chest bare but for two leather straps that held a quiver of arrows and a sword across his back. Close up, the Naga man's face was less human than Phoenix remembered. High cheekbones swept up to a narrow forehead and glossy, sleek black hair. Narrow, slanted eyes with no lashes or eyebrows were dominated by large, slitted, black irises. His skin was faintly bluish and the tips of two fangs stuck out over his thin bottom lip. Without changing expression, the Naga flicked a blue, forked tongue toward the prisoners, as though tasting their scent. He nodded to Bhumaka, whose smile deepened. Bhumaka nodded in turn to the tall Indian, who bowed and vanished out through the back tent-flap.

Phoenix tensed, still on his knees, awaiting Cadoc's signal. Clearly their disguise had been broken. The Naga went on scent, not sight, to identify people. Whatever Cadoc intended to do, he'd better do it soon – before Bhumaka called in soldiers to restrain them again.

When he did move, Cadoc took them all by surprise. Leaping up, he snatched a plate of hot curry sauce and flung it in the face of the Naga. The snake-man hissed, blinded and unable to retaliate. Bhumaka shouted in alarm. Everything seemed to happen at once. Phoenix spun on one knee as a guard came running into the tent, spear at the ready. Reaching up, Phoenix grabbed the wooden shaft, turned again. He used the guard's own forward momentum and tight grip on the weapon to hurl him onto the low table. Plates went flying in all directions. Food scattered over the bright cloths and cushions. The guard slid across the table, careening into Bhumaka and knocking him to the ground.

A second guard came in. Brynn stuck out a foot and tripped him. Marcus scrambled to his feet and smashed a large, pottery wine jug over the man's head as he fell. Red wine cascaded to the floor, spraying like blood.

At the same time, Cadoc made his big play. He snatched the boy, Nahapana, up under one arm. Yanking the child's belt-dagger free of its sheath, he held it to the small throat. The boy stopped struggling, his eyes huge with fear.

"Tell Bhumaka that I'll kill his son unless he returns all our gear and gives us safe passage north across the river."

"*Cadoc!*" Jade exclaimed.

"Now is not the time to get squeamish, Jade. I'm not going to hurt him but his father doesn't know that. Just tell him," Cadoc insisted, his eyes fixed on the Kshatrapa.

Phoenix held the tip of the guard's spear at the Naga's throat, ready to drive the point in should the snake-man even twitch wrong. Marcus stood near the tent flap, holding the other spear and awaiting more guards, should they come in. Brynn snatched up the child's bow and an arrow from the Naga sheath. He held it notched and ready, pointed at Bhumaka's heart. Jade translated.

Bhumaka climbed back to his feet and brushed his clothes down calmly. He looked at his son and nodded, acknowledging the boy's bravery.

"Very well, woman. Tell your companion you will get what you ask for if my son is returned immediately."

Jade translated and Cadoc shook his head. "No way. When we get over the river, we'll send him back and not any sooner."

Bhumaka's eyes narrowed but he nodded. "Very well. You have my word; the word of a Kshatrapa is law. You will not be detained – unless you harm my son."

"Deal," Cadoc agreed as Jade translated again. He grinned.

Phoenix gave him a reluctant nod. Taking a hostage wasn't a path he would have thought of himself but Cadoc had been right. It looked like they were going to be given safe passage without any bloodshed.

CHAPTER TEN

"I can't hold this much longer," Jade whispered to Phoenix as they rode slowly northeast through the camp.

When they left the pavilion, all their gear was waiting – including Blódbál, strapped to one of the horses' saddles. Phoenix snatched it out with a cry of delight and ran his hand lovingly down the flat of the blade, feeling its heat in his blood. Everything they had lost was there, intact. Marcus found this highly suspicious and so did Jade but Phoenix and Cadoc were determined to see it as a victory over Bhumaka.

Now they rode through the massed army of the Kshatrap, with Nahapana sitting before Cadoc, a knife still pressed to his throat. Word spread like wildfire through the army and everywhere they went, all eyes were on them. Silence swept before them and shocked whispers rose behind like a wave as they passed.

They rode in close formation, rubbing knees and flanks in an attempt to make it easier for Jade. Phoenix could see that she trembled with the effort of holding both their illusions and the largest shield spell she'd ever attempted. Bhumaka's guards sent a volley of arrows at their backs as they rode away from his tent. Only her quick casting saved Cadoc from instant death. Now, she clearly struggled to maintain a large, domed shield over all her companions and their horses. As they rode, the invisible bubble tumbled people aside, adding to the fear and awe their exploit generated.

Brynn, however, couldn't stop laughing at the sight.

"Not much further," Phoenix encouraged her. "We're almost at the edge of the camp."

"I can't do it!" she cried. "I have to let the illusion go or I'll lose the shield. Even then I'll only be able to hold it for a few more minutes – not long enough to get us across the river."

"Alright," he reached a quick decision, "lose the disguises but keep the shield as long as you can. Narrow it down to Cadoc and we'll all make a run for it. Wait until I give the signal, though." He called out in the Breton language. "Cadoc, we need a ford to get across the river. Think you can find one?"

The Player nodded, glancing around to get his bearings. His eyes glazed over as he switched out of his character and into the real world to Google the answer. Phoenix kept a close eye on him, hoping his digital body would react normally if something happened. He wasn't too sure what the program was designed to do with the character if a Player wasn't actually controlling it in the game.

Within moments, Cadoc returned. He grinned over his shoulder. "We're only about a kilometre from the river. It should be wide and shallow just over there." He pointed east.

"Right," Phoenix acknowledged. "On my signal, Jade, you drop the illusion and everyone ride as fast as you can for the river. If we can outdistance them it will give us time to get across without becoming pincushions."

Before them, the crowd of curious Indian soldiers thinned. Behind, the press of bodies made it difficult for the elite Saka troops to push through. It was now or never.

"Now!" he shouted, kicking his horse's flanks hard.

The stallion leapt forward at the same time as Jades' mare. She let the illusion go. Around them, Indians gasped in shock. Fingers pointed; cries of astonishment rang out. There was a brief, purple-blue flicker as her shield condensed around Cadoc and the princeling. Phoenix hoped the Saka would think it still protected all of them and not bother wasting more arrows.

All seven horses plunged ahead. Screams arose as Indian soldiers shoved back against each other, trying to get out of the way. Phoenix gritted his teeth against the awful noises and urged his mount onward. Then they were free and galloping wildly across the ploughed fields. Not far away, the river sparkled in the morning sun. Could they make it before the Saka caught up?

Grinning with mad excitement, Phoenix glanced behind. The smile slipped from his face. Racing toward them were fifty or more Saka warriors, bent low over their horses' necks, closing the gap rapidly. A dozen stood in their stirrups and drew bows, still galloping full tilt.

He swore and ducked, wishing for his long-lost shield as a volley of arrows sailed through the blue sky toward him. Most of them missed. One of them hit Marcus' packhorse in the rump, making the beast squeal and leap forward.

They plunged down a small embankment and splashed into the shallow river without slowing. It was a dangerous manoeuvre – there could be unseen deep water and holes in the riverbed. The water, cold from the mountains, splashed up, steaming off the hot flanks of the struggling horses. They were almost halfway across the ford before the sound of cursing and neighing from behind told them their pursuers had reached the rivers' edge.

Phoenix tried watch behind and ahead at the same time, expecting another flight of arrows in his back at any point. They were effectively trapped. There was no way they could escape being mowed down. Why had Cadoc suggested this? It was stupid to try and ride across a river with the enemy right on your heels.

The rain of death didn't come. Why? The Saka must know by now that Jade's shield was down. They must know that Nahapana was safe. Why didn't they just kill everyone else and take Cadoc down when he was alone?

Ahead, Jade cried out something incomprehensible and pointed toward the opposite bank. Phoenix looked up through a spray of water. Lining the levee on the north bank stood rank upon rank of mounted soldiers. Somehow, the Saka army had got across first and waited for them. His heart sank.

Glancing behind, he saw the soldiers on the south bank stop and retreat back to dry land. They shook their drawn weapons and shouted threats across the river; but why? The men ahead simply stared impassively at their counterparts, bows drawn, unmoving.

Jade's horse was the first to reach land. She spun the mare and the others followed her out of the water. Everyone was, amazingly enough, unharmed.

Cadoc grinned triumphantly over at her, his arm still clamping the boy to his chest. Nahapana blinked, eyes frightened in his small face.

"That must be Guatamiputra's army." Cadoc nodded to the row of soldiers standing above them on the riverbank. "We're safe for now. Let's go meet Guatamiputra and show him our prize." He hauled on the reins, turning his horse away from the river.

"Letta!" Jade yelled. The horse whickered in surprise as it stopped in its own tracks. Cadoc slewed around in his saddle and frowned at her.

"What're you doing? Let's go."

"We are *not* taking an innocent boy into the camp of his father's worst enemy," she said.

Brynn and Marcus drew their horses alongside hers, silently supporting her.

Phoenix moved his horse into a position between both sides, not really sure which to support.

"But it makes sense to hang on to him for awhile," Cadoc reasoned. "Guatamiputra will think we're spies but if we bring the boy he'll know we're on his side and he'll let us go free."

"You're probably right," Jade agreed, "but I'm still not doing it. It was bad enough that we used him as a hostage to get ourselves out of Bhumaka's camp. I'm not going to put him in any more danger. Set him down."

"What?" The Player raised his brows in wonder. "You're going to give up our best bargaining tool and walk into Guatamiputra's camp with nothing? We'll end up in exactly the same situation as before."

"No." She shook her head. "Bhumaka was acting on behalf of our Quest-enemy. Guatamiputra isn't."

"As far as you know," Cadoc pointed out. "It makes no sense in this game to give away such a big advantage. You'll lose. Phoenix, tell her."

"I dunno." Phoenix shrugged. It was a tricky situation and he wasn't sure who to back. "You could be right but so could she. It doesn't seem like the right thing to do."

"The right thing to do?" The warrior stared at Phoenix in amazement. "That doesn't matter here. You do what it takes to win, that's the right thing to do."

"I don't care," Jade said through gritted teeth. "I won't win by being underhanded."

"Well then, you'll lose," Cadoc stated flatly.

Phoenix glanced back and forth between Jade and Cadoc, not certain what to do. This was one of those situations his father had always tried to coach him for. He had to make the correct choice but what was it?

Cadoc was right: if they let Nahapana go, they lost a huge advantage over Bhumaka and a big bargaining chip with Guatamiputra. They could hand the Indian king the key to winning this war. Hadn't Jade said he was the true king? Wouldn't it also then be the right thing to help the true ruler win his war and restore the balance of power here? If they gave the boy to Guatamiputra, the war would be over and they could walk right into Pune and finish this level easily. Jade wanted to go home. Surely she couldn't disagree with a course of action that got her there faster?

On the other hand, surely it was the wrong thing to use a child as a pawn in a war?

But wasn't their survival more important than his?

Phoenix sighed and scraped his long hair back. "I'm probably going to regret this but I agree with Jade. Put the boy down and let him go back across the river to his father."

Cadoc shook his head and made a sound of disbelief. "You're mad, Phoenix. This could cost you the level, you know. Well, your call, I guess." He turned and lowered the boy to the ground.

Jade swung down from her mare, knelt in front of him and laid a hand on his shoulder.

"I'm sorry we had to use you that way. Thankyou for being so brave. Can you make it back across the river on your own? It's not very deep."

Nahapana drew himself up and nodded regally. With a scornful glance at Cadoc, he spun on his heel and marched straight into the cold waters without flinching. Stiff-backed, he pushed through the rushing rapids until he reached his own people. Their leader hauled the boy up on his horse and shook his fist at them before wheeling his mount and galloping away in a cloud of dust.

"I still say you're insane," Cadoc said. "After all, Bhumaka didn't keep his word about not harming us, so why should we keep ours?"

"Actually," Marcus murmured, "he only promised not to detain us. He never said anything about not harming us."

Brynn snorted at Cadoc's look of blank surprise. Phoenix glanced at Jade. She sent him a warm, grateful smile. Suddenly, he felt a small weight lift off his shoulders. Not only had he made the right choice for his team but he'd also been *asked* by his team to make that choice at the crucial moment. Perhaps they were finally coming to see him as a leader… and maybe he was finally starting to think like one. He just hoped it really was the right decision.

Without further conversation, they kicked their mounts back into action and rode up the embankment to meet their rescuers.

A tall, handsome Indian man rode forward and bowed his head. His eyes widened briefly at the sight of Jade's pale skin and white-blonde hair but he managed to hide his reaction quickly enough.

"Greetings from his Majesty, Raj Guatamiputra Satarkani. You will accompany me to express your gratitude to him in person. I am Vasisthiputra Pulamāvi, second son to his Majesty."

As soon as he heard the translation from Jade, Cadoc kneed his horse forward and inclined his head and gestured for Jade to join him.

"Greetings, your highness and thankyou for your timely intervention. I am Cadoc, Prince of the Dobunnic territories, *first* son of Corio, the King." He waved at the others. "We accept your invitation to exchange greetings with his Majesty. Pray, lead on."

Phoenix seethed inwardly. It annoyed him that Cadoc had simply taken over without consulting anyone else. He kept his mouth shut, though, because it was clear that little speech had made a positive impression on the Indian prince. Vasisthiputra gestured to his troop to form a guard around his prisoners but then rode beside Cadoc, keeping his sword sheathed and making polite conversation through Jade as though he were an honoured guest.

It didn't take long before they reached the outskirts of the kings' massive army, encamped on the vast, treeless plain north of the river. Phoenix caught Marcus' faintly impressed expression as they rode in. This army was a far cry from the disorderly hodgepodge of Bhumaka's camp. Here, he got the instant sense of organisation, efficiency and discipline. Everywhere he looked, Phoenix saw groups of men drilling for war: swordfighting; using spears; archery and formation riding. Huge, wood-and-iron four-wheeled battle-chariots, pulled by four horses and carrying three or four men raced each other on a long track. Nearby, elephants were being made ready for battle – their tusks sharpened and their armour polished. Soldiers looked fit, well-fed and skilled; their dhoti and turbans clean and whole. As well as swords, spears and bows, most carried a *katar* – a kind of short sword with a horizontal grip that placed the blade over the knuckles and allowed the user to deliver a fatal punch to his opponent.

By the time they reached Guatamiputra's tent, Phoenix was pretty sure they were dealing with a skilled general. He was glad they had let Nahapana go. This Raj didn't need to hold a child hostage to win a war.

Vasisthiputra dismounted and politely, but firmly, requested they leave their weapons in the hands of the guards outside. Reluctantly, Phoenix parted with his sword once more. This was happening far too often. Brynn handed over his belt knife then, when the guard eyed him steadily, sighed and added his sling to the pile.

The Indian prince preceded them into the large pavilion. The inside could not have been a more marked contrast to Bhumaka's. Not a silken drape nor gaudy cushion in sight. Straight-backed wooden chairs surrounded a large, rectangular table. Around this sat five older men, all of whom carried themselves with the authority of age and experience. At the head of the table stood a mature version of Vasisthiputra: tall and handsome but with grey touching his temple. Guatamiputra. Beside him slouched a richly-dressed young man about the same age as Vasisthiputra. He wore a disgruntled, irritated expression on his aristocratic face that immediately, and for no real reason, annoyed Phoenix.

The men looked up at their entrance and all rose to their feet as Vasisthiputra explained the situation. Guatamiputra eyed the outlanders thoughtfully, leaning with his knuckles on the table. He looked intelligent but very tired.

"Is this true? Were you truly escaping from my enemy's camp? Or are you spies sent by him? Where are you from? Who was the child you returned across the river?" He demanded.

Jade translated rapidly in a low undertone, for Cadoc's sake but Phoenix stepped forward to speak.

He bowed. "My lord, we are travellers from a distant land. We are simply passing through your country, seeking to complete a task that has nothing to do with you or with your enemies. We were captured by Bhumaka and, in seeking to escape, we held his son hostage temporarily. True to our word, we released the boy as soon as we were safely out of Bhumaka's reach."

Guatamiputra gazed narrowly at them, one at a time, assessing the truth of the story.

"And this task you must complete," he asked, "where must you go for that?"

"To Pune…um…I mean, Punya-Vishaya, my lord," Phoenix replied.

The Raj straightened. "To Punya-Vishaya? But the town is held by Bhumaka. How do you propose to get in there and complete your task if you have made an enemy of him?"

Phoenix grinned and gave a one-shouldered shrug. "We hadn't quite worked that one out yet. In fact, our planning didn't go much past getting over the river. It was just luck that your son and his men happened to be there."

Guatamiputra raised an eyebrow. "A good general does not rely on luck. Vasi was there because he is a valiant warrior and I sent him there to watch the enemy." He turned away and caught sight of the other young man, who stared at Jade with outright greed. Guatimputra sighed.

"My first son, Sopaniputra, however, prefers to recite poetry to women."

The young man started then glared at his father before schooling his face into blankness.

The Raj turned away and paced over to a low wooden shrine that was set into one corner of the tent. He stood, staring down at it for several moments before moving aside. Phoenix heard Jade gasp and stole a quick look at the shrine. He couldn't see anything particularly remarkable about it. It was just a decorative niche in which sat a small statue of a man with blue skin and four arms. Each of the hands held something but the details were too small to make out exactly what. He would have to ask her what she had seen, later.

"And your names?" the Raj shot at them.

Phoenix introduced them, this time using their real names. Remembering the effect Cadoc's princely status had on Vasisthiputra, he added both his and Jade's titles.

"This is Prince Cadoc, first son of King Corio of the Dobunnic territories."

Guatamiputra raised his eyebrows and nodded politely.

"And this is her royal highness, Jade gan Eleri, daughter of Arawn, king of the Elves," Phoenix concluded, hoping for a slightly better result.

He wasn't even sure if Elves were part of Indian mythology but they needed every bit of influence they could get over this man if they were to achieve their goal of returning the Sudarshana to Pune in time for the last night of the old moon. They had already lost two of the six nights Anuket had given them to complete the task.

Guatamiputra's reaction was everything Phoenix could have wished. He paled then flushed dark, leaning on the table to support himself as if suddenly weakened. His eyes sparkled with excitement, as did those of his advisors.

"It is you, then," he said softly, staring at Jade in fascination. "You are the *Devi*, the daughter of the Gods, the Shining One destined to restore my kingdom to me. You have come. I just never expected you to be a woman."

Jade blinked at him, clearly taken aback. The Raj smiled broadly and threw one arm around Sopaniputra's shoulders and the other around hers. She flinched at the touch of his leather and iron wristband.

"Come!" the king squeezed them both, "we shall have a banquet to celebrate this special event."

Phoenix exchanged confused looks with Marcus and Brynn.

"Err…, your majesty?" he asked. "What special event is that?"

The Raj laughed heartily. "The marriage of my son to this Princess of the Elves, of course. With her in our family, my victory is assured!"

CHAPTER ELEVEN

"No!" "What!?" Phoenix, Jade, Marcus and Brynn all spoke at once.

Marcus stepped up and dragged Jade out from beneath the Raj's arm. Phoenix and Brynn moved to stand protectively before her. Guatamiputra's son, Sopaniputra, scowled. Several of the Raj's advisors jumped to their feet and cast outraged, venomous looks at them. If weapons had been allowed in the room, they would already have come to blows. The tension was thick enough to cut. Vasisthiputra waved them back, frowning at the foreigners.

Guatamiputra drew himself up. "Who do you think you are? She may be a *devi* but she is still just a woman. She is beautiful and of royal blood – a perfect match for my son and heir. I demand that you give her to me."

Behind, Phoenix heard Jade sputtering with indignation. He needed to cool things down before she lost her temper and *Commanded* the Raj to do something embarrassing. Phoenix held up both hands, trying to placate the man.

"I'm sorry, my lord. In our country, women are not property or slaves. Jade has her own mind. If she wants to marry your son, of course she can but nobody will make her as long as we're around."

Jade folded her arms and sent the Raj and Sopaniputra a narrow look, as if daring them to try something. Cadoc muttered in her ear, demanding a translation. She flushed pink but gave him a brief synopsis. He grinned.

The Raj stared at them, clearly taken aback. Sopaniputra tugged on his sleeve but Guatamiputra brushed him away. With a sigh, he waved them all to sit down.

"Sit down, sit down. I'm not going to have you killed for defying me." He frowned at them. "Not yet, anyway. My wife tells me the tradition of arranging marriages for our daughters is a recent invention, so I suppose I should not be surprised that other cultures do not follow it."

The groups sat, watching each other warily. Phoenix sent Jade a warning frown and she huffed back at him, unfolding her arms and sitting down with a thump.

"So if she is not to marry my son and bring her Elven kin to save my kingdom, then how is she to fulfil her destiny?" The Raj demanded.

"Um," Jade put up a hand.

The Raj raised haughty brows at her then sighed again. "Speak then, woman. I suppose I must get used to the idea. I just hope my wife and daughters don't get to hear of this."

Behind him, Vasisthiputra covered his mouth to hide a smile.

"I don't think my Elven father would come to your rescue, anyway," Jade admitted. "I don't know him very well, you see, since I was raised amongst humans. But I am a Spellweaver," she added, when the Raj looked disappointed. "Maybe we can come to some sort of deal?"

"Deal?" The Raj blinked at her in astonishment. "You want to bargain with me, woman?"

Jade shrugged. "It's only fair. I'm sure we can come up with a good plan to defeat Bhumaka using the skills we have between us. We help you to regain your kingdom, you help us complete our quest once you've retaken Punya-Vishaya. The only condition is that we have just four days to do it. We have to be in Punya-Vishaya by the last night of the moon."

For a long moment, the Raj looked at her and the rest

of the companions. Then he grimaced. "I suppose that will have to do. For a moment I thought I'd found a way to avoid this war altogether. I guess a short one is better than a war that drags on for weeks."

He stood abruptly and everyone scrambled to their feet. "You are tired. Tonight we will celebrate your long-awaited arrival and tomorrow we will plan the defeat of Bhumaka." He clapped his hands. Three women scurried into the pavilion, bright sari's fluttering like butterfly wings.

"Take them to the guest quarters and see they are rested and fittingly dressed for tonight's banquet." He waved his hands in dismissal and turned away. Vasisthiputra jerked his head at them, indicating they should follow the women.

Relieved, the companions retreated. Guatamiputra was a bewildering mix of vibrant, charismatic leader and cultural mysteries that made no sense to them. For several tense minutes, Phoenix had been sure they would be executed on the spot. He was surprised to find the Raj so open to challenge and suggestion.

Vasisthiputra walked with them to the men's tent. Phoenix protested when Jade was towed off to a different one.

"Hey, Prince Vasisthi…thithputra." He stumbled over the name as he tried to watch where Jade was going.

"She will not be harmed. The women will take her bathe and be dressed for tonight's welcoming banquet," the prince said, smiling. "Please, call me Vasi."

"I don't get it." Phoenix frowned at him. "Why do you all keep talking about a welcoming feast as though you knew we were coming?"

Vasi blinked at him. "But we did know."

Now it was Phoenix's turn to blink. "Huh?"

"The coming of the Shining One has been foretold for years," the prince said. "Not the exact date, of course – and we are a bit surprised to find she is a woman."

"And what's this 'Shining One' supposed to do?" Phoenix asked, not sure he really wanted to know the answer.

"The prophecy is painted on the walls of the Pataleshwar cave temple in Punya-Vishaya. It shows a war being fought on the plains outside the town. High above, there is an eagle, soaring through the sky. On its back is the white *devi* – holding high the lost Silver Sudarshana." Vasi waved his hands around, demonstrating as he spoke.

Phoenix exchanged alarmed glances with Marcus. Brynn, who was grudgingly translating for Cadoc, broke off and gaped at them in astonishment.

"The…er…*lost* Sudarshana, you say," Phoenix tried to sound casual. "And exactly what is this Sudarshana. What does it do?"

Vasi frowned. "It is a weapon of sorts. A tool of the great god, Brahma. In his aspect as the *devi* Vishnu, the Preserver of the World, he carries with him four items: a mace, a lotus flower, a conch shell and a chakra. Many years ago, Vishnu chose to come to earth and his avatar lived amongst humans, doing great things with his chosen tools."

The prince went on, explaining who the god Vishnu was and what each tool represented. Phoenix, who had jumped at the word 'avatar', quickly realised that it didn't quite mean the same thing as it did in the modern world. Here, 'avatar' literally meant a god who took human form. It was a very weird coincidence, though.

"Vishnu is just one aspect of the great god, Brahman. Vishnu is the master of the past, present and future; the creator and destroyer of all existences," Vasi said, obviously trying to put difficult concepts of the Hindu religion into simple words. "The Conch shell represents Vishnu's creativity – the creation of the five elements: water, earth, air, fire and sky. The Mace represents the primeval force from which all mental and physical strength comes. The Lotus stands for freedom, knowledge and truth underlying all things. The Chakra, named 'Sudarshana', literally means 'good vision' – or the ability to see yourself clearly." Vasi continued. "The one in Punya-Vishaya has been missing from its place in the statue of Vishnu in the cave-temple for three years. Legend says it is *the* Sudarshana – the one Vishnu himself used. Since it has been gone, my family has lost more and more of our kingdom to the Saka invaders. Our family has ruled wisely and justly for many years. We need to reclaim what is ours; to restore the balance of power here so the people do not suffer any longer under foreign rule. That is why we need the Sudarshana."

Phoenix interrupted. "So you're saying this missing Sudarshana has what, the ability to make people see themselves clearly? How is that a weapon?"

Vasi turned a clear, dark-eyed gaze on him. "It is like a mirror for the soul. Are you prepared to see what is in the darkest corners of your heart? Are you so pure that you can face every decision you've made without flinching? Are you so perfect that you always do the right thing; always choose the right path; always speak and think with humble gratitude and compassion? Are you never guilty of selfishness, ego or greed?"

He paused as Phoenix digested his words then continued. "If you are then you have nothing to fear from the Sudarshana. Here is your tent. I will send someone for you when the feast begins." Bowing, he turned on his heel and strode away, leaving the companions in stunned silence.

When they got inside, Cadoc flung himself down on some cushions and sighed.

"So what was all that he said at the end? The boy stopped translating. You all seemed pretty impressed by it. What was it? Something about the wedding? Maybe Jade should just marry the guy to save all this drama. She could probably help more from the inside, anyway."

Brynn slipped past, giving Phoenix a cool look. "*The boy,* has a name," he muttered in the Svear language, "and *the boy* didn't think his highness needed to know about the Sudarshana. *The boy* also thinks his highness should keep his stupid opinions to himself."

Phoenix opened his mouth to rebuke Brynn for being cheeky but shut it again. Brynn was right but maybe not for the reasons he thought. He was obviously jealous of Cadoc's friendship with Jade and therefore didn't like the Prince. Phoenix was more worried that a discussion of the Sudarshana might accidentally draw out details of their Quest – which might, in turn, lead to one of them being deleted from the game.

Instead, he spoke to Brynn in the same language. "Jade needs to know about this stuff. Do you think you can find her and fill her in?"

The boy nodded, inspecting a star-fruit before taking a cautious nibble and talking around it. "Should I warn her not to tell princey-boy here?"

Phoenix glanced at Cadoc. The Player frowned at him, clearly not happy that they were excluding him from the conversation. Well, he'd just have to accept that they couldn't discuss their Quest in front of him.

"Yes," Phoenix agreed, "you'd better, just in case. Just tell her she'll know why. Oh, and tell her we need a plan to defeat Bhumaka's army, too."

*****

Jade sat in solitary splendour in the luxury of the 'women's tent', feeling stunned. As soon as she had reached it a gaggle of women had rushed out to embrace her and touch her face and hair. Helpless, she had been swept off by the king's wife and daughters to be bathed and pampered until she was ready to scream.

Now, they had finally left her alone for a few minutes

and she had no idea what to do. If she moved, something might get dislodged. They had taken off her travel-stained rough clothes and dressed her like a doll in a leaf-green sari exquisitely embroidered with silver and gold thread. Her hands and feet were decorated with red-brown henna in intricate patterns that defied analysis. Her throat, hands, arms and hair were bedecked in so much silver jewellery that she was scared to move in case she fell over with the weight. They had even put thick, dark kohl around her eyes and a red stain of some sort on her lips.

Gnawing on her reddened bottom lip, she resigned herself to a period of waiting. She propped her chin on her hand. Bracelets clattered down her arm. From the chatter of the women as they dressed her, she had gathered the basics of what was painted on the walls of the temple in Punya-Vishaya but it worried her. How could she possibly be the centre of some sort of ancient prophecy? How was she supposed to ride an eagle? What sort of weapon was the Sudarshana and how was she supposed to use it? Was she supposed to fling it like some magic Frisbee? Who was this Vishnu god guy, anyway?

Thinking back to Anuket's instructions when the goddess handed them the silver chakra in Egypt, Jade frowned. Anuket had said '….*a path will be taken that will make whole what is torn asunder; he who has wronged will be redeemed and an Empire will unite.*' The Empire must be Guatamiputra's, that was obvious but who had done something wrong and what had been torn asunder?

All she knew was that the Sudarshana had to be returned to its rightful owner. Sudden panic struck and Jade struggled to her feet. Trailing lengths of green silk, she went to the neat pile of her things the women had left. Her seeking fingers found the Hyllion Bagia and she sighed in relief. It was safe. She tucked it and her life-dagger into her sari and carefully sat down again on a pile of gaudy cushions.

The statue in Guatamiputra's tent must have been an image of this Vishnu guy, since it held a miniature chakra in one of its blue hands. Obviously the Sudarshana was too big to go on *that* statue but somewhere in Pune, there must be a big, four-armed, blue-skinned guy who was missing a chakra. She just had to find it. Maybe it was in the same temple as the painting about her and the eagle…?

An odd, hissing sound coming from outside the tent distracted her. It sounded like a gas leak but that was obviously impossible. She heard her name called and realised Brynn lurked somewhere close by. Scrambling over to the tent wall, she whispered to him.

"Brynn? Are you ok?"

"I'm fine," he said, "how about you? What are they doing?"

"Nothing now," she replied testily. "But I've been scrubbed clean and dressed in the most ridiculous outfit you've ever seen. They've even put makeup on me!"

Brynn giggled. "Nice to know you're not being tortured, anyway."

"That's a matter of opinion," she retorted. "What's going on with you?"

"We're fine, too. We're being treated like royalty, actually. Food everywhere – as long as you can eat the spicy stuff they make here. The fruit's funny-shaped, too."

"Oh do shut up about food and tell me what been going on," she interrupted.

"Well," he mused, "Cadoc thinks you should go through with the wedding to keep the king on our side but Phoenix heard from Vasi that the Sudarshana is a weapon you need to wield in battle against the Saka."

"Yes, I know that," Jade said impatiently.

"You do?"

"These women gossip something terrible," she sighed. "What else?"

"Phoenix says you shouldn't talk to Cadoc about the

Sudarshana – he says you'll know why."

"I will?" She thought for a moment. "Oh, yes. OK. What else?"

"Er…he says can you please come up with a plan for defeating Bhumaka's army while you're at it."

"Great," she groaned, "business as usual, I see."

"Good," the boy agreed, her irony lost on him. "I'll go tell the others you're going to come up with something."

Before Jade could reply, there was a soft scuffling as Brynn slipped away. Huffing, she sat down with her back to one of the tent poles and folded her arms.

"Fabulous. OK. I'll work on that. You guys just chat amongst yourselves and leave it all to me then." Her sarcasm fell on heedless tent walls. "Honestly. Men!"

CHAPTER TWELVE

Phoenix paced the huge tent, awaiting Brynn's return. The boy had a perfect genius for sliding away unnoticed. The guards posted outside their door had not even seen him slip under a sidewall and disappear into the crowds. Of course, it helped that he now looked very much like any other small boy wandering about the camp.

After agreeing to go find Jade, Brynn had been quick to change into the clothing provided by their host. Then he'd smudged every inch of exposed skin with dirt and charcoal from the fire until he looked like a gutter brat. Finally, he slid under the canvas wall and vanished. Now they were awaiting his return and hoping no-one visited them in the meantime. He was small but they were sure to notice his absence.

There was a rustling at the back of the tent and Brynn's grubby face poked under the cloth. Grinning, he rolled in the rest of the way and stood up, brushing himself off as he swaggered over.

"Why bother?" Marcus raised an ironic eyebrow at his filthy state.

"Hey," the boy shrugged, "if you don't want to know how she is, that's fine with me."

Marcus smiled. "You found her. I'm impressed. Tell us."

Brynn lay back on a pile of cushions, interlaced his hands behind his head and shrugged. "She's complaining about being dressed up and made up like a doll but otherwise she's fine. She'd already heard the legend and she's agreed not to talk and to come up with a plan to defeat Bhumaka."

"Bet she didn't say it like that." The Roman's sly comment went unheeded.

Cadoc stretched and sat up. "Why bother helping this Raj against Bhumaka? Why not just complete your quest now? You don't owe him anything. I'm pretty close to completing mine, so why don't we just ditch these guys and head to Pune now?"

"Our quest has to be completed on a specific day." Phoenix sighed, scratching his fingers over his scalp. "We've got to wait a few more days before we can do what we came to do. I have a feeling this war isn't going to wait that long."

"You go ahead, though," Brynn put in brightly. "Feel free to leave us behind if we're slowing you down."

The Player sent him a scornful look. "As if I'd do that. You guys are in a tight spot and if I can help, I will. Why don't we see if we can come up with a plan, too."

There was a scratching at the tent door and the flap opened to admit Vasi. Behind him came a vision that put a stop to conversation: Jade. When she glided in, even Phoenix blinked, temporarily struck dumb. Cadoc scrambled to his feet, stammering a greeting. Marcus said nothing but his handsome face flushed and he clenched his fists. Lifting the hem of her green silk sari, Jade stepped delicately toward them, her eyes huge and brilliantly emerald. Her hands were intricately decorated with what looked like reddish tattoos. Part of the sari was draped over her head, framing her delicate face and making her curled blonde hair almost glow.

She was beautiful. There was no other word for it: except, perhaps, 'exquisite' and all the other similar adjectives he could think of. Phoenix remembered he had originally thought them when he'd first met her avatar as a Player, playing the game from outside. So much had happened since that he'd just become used to her smart, sarcastic, cautious personality and forgotten her looks altogether.

He said the first thing that popped into his head. "It might be a good idea to get changed back into your own clothes if you really don't want to marry this Sopaniputra guy. He'll probably have a fit if he sees you like this."

Jade frowned at him for a moment then smiled. "Why Phoenix, I think that was sort of a compliment."

She then turned the full force of that smile on Vasi and laid a hand on his arm. "Thank you so much for bringing me to my friends. Would you mind if we had a few minutes to talk?"

Vasi stared at her for a moment then shook himself and bowed. "Of course, my lady. When you are ready, call and you will all be escorted to the feast."

When he left, Jade turned back to her friends, and Phoenix caught a faint, satisfied, almost smug expression on her face. He had the distinct feeling that she was happy with the impression she'd made on the men. His real-world family hadn't prepared him for how to deal with sisters but in this world he had two sisters and several memories of their flirting efforts with his friends made him uncomfortable. He hoped she'd go back to her normal clothes soon. It was distracting to have her dressed up. She could have pushed the others over with a blown kiss.

"I wanted to talk to you about the war," she said, turning serious. "There's a new problem. The Saka evidently use poisoned arrows."

"How did you find that out?" Phoenix dropped back onto the cushions, relieved she'd changed the subject.

Jade paced the floor, jingling with each step. "Vasi told me one of our packhorses died from an arrowshot."

Marcus jumped, looking guilty. She hastened to

reassure him.

"It was such a shallow wound that the Horsemaster didn't think it was worth telling us about. There's no way you could have known about the poison, Marcus."

The Roman shrugged and they all sat down amongst the cushions. "So how does this affect plans for the battle?"

"Well, there's no way I can heal hundreds of poisoned troops or shield them from thousands of arrows," she said matter-of-factly. "So we're going to have to come up with some way of protecting people against the poison."

"I thought Elven magic didn't work against iron weapons anyway," Cadoc said.

Jade shrugged. "Mine does, to a limited extent, because I'm a half-elf but I don't think I could hold against a whole lot of iron weapons in one spot at once."

Cadoc nodded his understanding. He was busy brewing a pot of tea over the small, central hearth fire. Handing Jade a cup and nodding to the others to help themselves, he yanked aside a rug and rubbed a flat patch in the dirt beneath. She took the tea with a grateful smile, warming her hands on the rough clay pot. Phoenix frowned at them, wondering whether Cadoc was more interested in Jade than he'd realised. He'd have to keep an eye on the Player.

Cadoc sipped his tea then drew some lines in the dirt. "I've been doing some research into ancient Indian war tactics."

Marcus and Brynn stared at him in astonishment, cups of tea halfway to their mouths. Luckily, Jade jumped in before they could ask the obvious question. They had no idea Cadoc was a Player with access to the Web in the real world.

"Great." She beamed at him with more brilliance than strictly necessary. "What did you find out?"

He promptly launched into a detailed discussion of war

tactics and battle formations. Before long, Marcus, Phoenix and Brynn were all hotly involved in debating various ideas. Phoenix and Cadoc were all for using a modern form guerrilla warfare but Marcus vetoed it on the basis that the flat, treeless terrain combined with the sheer size of the armies would make it ineffective as well as dishonourable. Phoenix saw Jade zone out when they started talking about the strategic use of elephants, chariots, infantry and cavalry. Cadoc went into great detail about the classic, standard formations that ancient Indian generals used to position their men – the lotus formation, the hawk formation, the chakra and the eagle formations.

"No!" Marcus sliced his hand through the air as though cutting Cadoc's words off. His uncharacteristic intensity startled even Jade out of her thoughts. "It would be stupid to use standard tactics and formations – that is exactly what Bhumaka will expect. He will be ready for them."

"He has a point," Phoenix conceded.

Cadoc pursed his lips, frowning then nodded. "OK, so what do you suggest? Roman tactics?"

"No," Marcus said evenly. "Roman battle plans are worked around smaller armies with experienced cavalry and better armour. The Indians seem to count on infantry numbers to win. With no way of communicating quickly, it is too hard to co-ordinate armies of this size in the same way. No, we need something simpler; a surprise." He stared at the floor for a moment then looked up. "Ballista."

"Bless you," Brynn said.

Marcus ignored him. "Or perhaps an onager would be simpler to build."

Jade nodded, apparently agreeing.

"What?" Phoenix cast a puzzled look at Marcus then at Brynn, who shrugged.

"Don't look at me, I thought he'd sneezed."

"They're both types of catapults," Marcus explained.

"Ballista are like giant crossbows and onager are like a giant version of a sling – they throw huge rocks at the enemy."

"If they've never been used in India, it will come as a big shock to Bhumaka's men," Cadoc sounded more enthusiastic.

"So now we just have to convince Guatamiputra to build whole lot of huge catapults, and train his men how to use them? All in two days." Phoenix rotated his neck and rubbed a hand over his face. He sighed, wishing for a miracle but unable to think of anything better. "Well, it's the best we've come up with so far. Who wants to convince the Raj?"

*****

It soon turned out that they would have to wait until morning to discuss anything more serious than the taste of roasted peacock with the Raj. The welcoming feast was so packed with people, ceremony, eating, dancing, a long and confusing morality play involving a multitude of gods and their interactions with humans, more ceremony and more eating; that it was impossible to hold a confidential conversation with him.

Long before midnight, Jade was heartily bored and totally exhausted. She'd never much liked parties but this was worse than most. As the 'Shining One' who was supposed to save them, she'd sort of expected a seat of honour and the royal treatment. It seemed, however, that being female outweighed being the potential bringer of victory. She sat several places away from Guatamiputra and his advisors, stuck between Brynn and Sopaniputra. She was also the only girl at the table who wasn't serving food.

Oh, and she'd had more than enough of the wrong sort of attention. So much, that she was fast beginning to regret her decision to wear the sari and makeup. Dozens of men stared openly at her, calling out sly, outrageous compliments on her beauty; talking to each other about her looks as though she was deaf and stupid. Nobody wanted to hold a serious conversation about anything important. When she tried, they just smiled patronisingly, or patted her hand and told her not to worry her pretty head about it. It was humiliating. She was rapidly coming to realise that being really beautiful wasn't as great she thought it would be, if it meant everyone thought you had nothing intelligent to say.

Brynn had been yawning his head off for hours and ignoring Jade's attempts to get him to go to bed. Sopaniputra, on the other hand, would not stop pestering her no matter how rude she was. He was arrogant beyond belief and obviously still deluding himself that she was, somehow, his property. Even worse, he insisted that she call him Sopan and kept expecting her to be thrilled to hear all about his life. It was dull. He was dull. She wanted to slap him and tell him to shut up and listen for a change.

Finally, infuriated by his self-centred attitude and inability to take a hint, Jade *Commanded* him under her breath. Seconds after she muttered *sleep*, the prince fell face-first into his dessert and began snoring.

Brynn nudged her and giggled. "Nice one."

She flushed and tried to look innocent as the prince's men carried him away. "I shouldn't have done it," she whispered. "We should probably get some sleep, too. I'm still not feeling a hundred percent and I'm sick of this party."

"You go ahead," he replied, yawning, "I want to see the fire-eaters."

"Fine," she growled. "If you're tired tomorrow, don't blame me."

Brynn grinned. "There you go again, sounding like my mother."

Jade made a sound of frustration and got up from the table. After untangling her sari from the chair, she glanced around. The others were all in deep conversation, so no-one else saw her leave. It was probably just as well; she was getting pretty tired of the 'fragile property' kind of treatment. The Indian men seemed to either view women as useless decoration or as slaves. If nothing else, she now had a new appreciation for the freedoms of modern women.

Holding her sari off the ground with one hand, she made her way through the gloom toward her tent. A thin anklet of bells tinkled irritatingly with every step she took. Overhead, a slice of the waning moon glowed silver in a star-spattered sky. All around were warm human and animal sounds of the army camp: sleepy mutterings, stomping of horse's hooves, jingling of the thin chains around the elephant's feet.

Jade was almost to her tent when a sudden change in her surroundings made her shiver and look up. Something wasn't right. A feeling of foreboding washed over her. Somewhere, very nearby, someone meant to do her no good. But where? Who?

Regretting that she'd left her staff with her gear, she slipped her dagger out and clutched it tightly. Her heart pounded as she considered her options. The feast fire was too far away for a quick dash to safety – not that she could run properly in this outfit, anyway. There was no guarantee a yell for help would alert friendly assistance, either. She had no way of knowing who was out there or why they bore her ill will. For all she knew, the whole army might be afraid of her, the way Bhumaka's men had been.

There was no time for more thought. Shadows rushed at her from four directions. Despairingly, Jade realised there were far too many of them for her to fend off with just one little dagger. Time to try something new.

Standing tall, she reached up toward the stars with one hand and pointed at her nearest attacker with the dagger. Closing her eyes, she yelled,

"Sky-hiti!"

From above came a *crack* of thunder that shook the ground. Through her eyelids, Jade saw a brilliant, purple-blue-white flash as the *'cloud-flame'* spell took effect and called lightning down from a cloudless sky. Screams told her she'd at least frightened the men. Smiling grimly, she opened her eyes. Half a dozen dark, still shapes sprawled around her. *That* should buy some time and summon help as well. Now to hold them off until someone came.

Clutching her little bronze knife, Jade cast a small shield spell around herself. It wouldn't hold for long. It was taking her body longer than she expected to recover from the drugged spices Leela had put in their food the night before, even with food and herbs.

More men poured out of the darkness, surrounding her; approaching more warily. She swallowed. She didn't have enough power left to draw lighting down on their heads again. Something simpler, then. Sweeping a finger in a circle that pointed at knee height, she muttered *collapse* under her breath. A dozen or more men staggered, stumbled and fell in helpless heaps on the ground. A dozen more stepped up to replace them, knives flashing in the moonlight.

Still no-one came to her rescue. Jade bit her lip. A teleportation spell would come in handy about now. Or even telepathy so she could mentally call for help. Wait! Maybe she could. Another spell from the Svear spellbook came to mind. It hadn't made sense at the time but maybe the words *heili-tala*, which translated as *'brain-talk'* meant some sort of telepathy. It was worth a try.

At that moment, her shield began to tremble under the impact of a dozen knives. She staggered and fell to her knees under the pressure of so much iron. She almost felt the sting of the metal on her own flesh and in her mind. Around her, silent, dark attackers pushed and twisted their metal death into her magic, draining it, sucking it away along with her very life force. Flickers of purple-blue sparks skittered along the blades. One or two men dropped their weapons and fled, muttering counter-curses as they ran. More replaced them.

She slipped further, curling into a ball to protect the Hyllion Bagia tucked into her sari. She sank to the cold ground, weakening with every second. Closer and closer the fatal circle came as her shield shrank, little by little, under the power of so much iron.

With the last of her strength, Jade silently mouthed the Svear spell. Unable to tell if it had worked, she cried out in her head. *'Phoenix! Help!'*

The little protective bubble burst and sharp, gleaming death descended. Her last conscious thought was that Phoenix would be so annoyed if he found her dead - again.

CHAPTER THIRTEEN

Phoenix was sleepily watching the fire-eating display when Brynn came up behind and tapped him on the shoulder.

The boy yawned. "I'm off to bed. Jade's already gone. See you in the morning." He gave Marcus a jaunty wave.

Looking up with a smile, Phoenix opened his mouth to say good-night but was silenced by a massive crack of thunder that sounded almost overhead. A brief flash of blinding, white-purple-blue light blazed across the camp at the same instant. Phoenix jumped to his feet, blinking away the spots that now danced in front of his eyes. Blódbál was already in his hand, although he didn't remember drawing it.

"Wow," Cadoc looked up at the clear night sky. "That was weird. There's not even any storm clouds. I didn't think you could get lightning without clouds. What do you reckon caused it?"

Marcus, Phoenix and Brynn looked at each other. "Jade."

Phoenix nodded.

At that moment, he heard her voice – in his head. The blank, worried look on Marcus' face told him no-one else had heard.

"Come on," he said in an undertone. "She's in trouble."

Without asking stupid questions, Marcus and Brynn fell into step beside him as he ran toward their tents. It took Cadoc a few seconds to realise they'd gone but he caught up quickly and drew his sword after one look at their grim expressions. Vasi slipped away from the feast and followed.

In the darkness between the tents, Phoenix saw shadows moving, clustering and pushing toward something on the ground in one great, heaving mass. With a wordless war-cry he charged, intent on scattering the group. He didn't want to start a battle if Jade wasn't even there and this was all some sort of mistake.

She was.

The men spread before his attack then regrouped around the pathetic little heap of green silk in their midst. Clad in black, with their faces darkened, it was impossible to recognise the assassins. It didn't really matter who they were, anyway. Blódbál was singing loud and Phoenix wasn't inclined to ignore the sword's encouragement this time. Anger swelled in his chest. Behind him, his companions raised their weapons and charged.

One after another, seven men fell as Cadoc flicked his throwing knives with deadly accuracy. More slipped out of the darkness, building a human wall between Jade and her rescuers. Who the hell were these guys? What did they want with her?

Phoenix snatched out his dagger and moved to join the fray. One man, taller and stronger-looking than the others, stepped forward to meet him. In one hand he held a small, circular shield, the other was empty. He glided sideways, drawing Phoenix away from the group. Teeth gleamed white in his masked face.

Phoenix hesitated, glancing at Jade and at his friends. Marcus, Cadoc and Brynn were making serious headway against their enemies. Brynn stood back, watching everything and using his sling with lethal, perfect precision.

Occasionally he called out a warning to Marcus or Cadoc if they were in danger. Marcus fought with his usual silent, flawless action. Cadoc was more flamboyant – laughing and calling out taunts to the assassins as he waded through them, blade flashing and eyes glittering. They seemed to be handling things pretty well.

All this, Phoenix took in at a quick glance. When he looked back, his opponent was no longer unarmed. He uncoiled a bizarre, five-foot long, flexible steel blade from around his waist, where he had apparently been wearing it like a belt. Phoenix stared in fascination as he pulled it free and swished it expertly through the air. It sliced the night with the clean, almost-musical sound of a razor-sharp blade.

Bemused, he watched as the assassin flicked and twisted the flexible steel around himself in a demonstration of incredible skill. How on earth did the man manage not to cut himself?   And how he could possibly hurt anyone else with such a bendy blade?

Then, suddenly, it was no longer a question of how but when. The dark assassin leaped forward with cat-like grace, whipping the sword overhead in an arc. Raising his arm automatically, Phoenix blocked the blow with Blódbál – and cried out in anger and pain as the supple steel bent over his own blade and sliced across his face.

Shocked, he jumped back, out of the long reach of his opponent.   He touched his cheek and felt the warm stickiness of blood. It stung! The assassin grinned again and dropped into a fighting crouch, circling to the left. Phoenix turned to follow his movements.

Fighting against an expert with this sword was not going to be a simple matter of combining Aikido and standard sword-fighting skills. His adversary had a much longer reach and was obviously not going to over-balance forward by thrusting or jabbing. The blade might not be able to impale Phoenix but it could certainly slice through a major artery with ease.

The man swung his blade in figure-of-eight arcs around himself, never taking his eyes off Phoenix. He edged forward. Phoenix moved back, trying to stay out of reach; looking for an opening; a weakness. The Indian leapt high, swinging his sword overhead at an angle. Phoenix spun aside, barely escaping being cut again as the metal swept past his ear. Again his attacker sprang, swinging the other way and turning in the air with unexpected agility. Again Phoenix escaped with bare millimetres to spare; unable to close the gap without exposing himself to that deadly cutting edge.

Blódbál's wordless tune of destruction sang in his head, growing louder and more insistent as frustration peaked. He pushed it aside, trying to stay calm. Getting angry would only cloud his thinking and this was one fight he really had to think his way out of. None of his usual tactics would work against this bizarre weapon. He had to come up with something new. But what?

Too late! His adversary was on him again. This time he twirled closer with a spinning kick, quickly followed with a wicked horizontal slash of the sword. Phoenix managed to turn aside from the kick. He thrust at an exposed leg but he misjudged the distance. The razor edge scored his back, leaving a fiery line of agony blazing across his ribs. Gasping, he staggered away, clutching at his side. Blood slid down his skin, warm and wet. He should have kept his leather armour on, rather than a silly silk dress shirt.

This was just not working. The black-clad assassin had a longer reach and was too quick and agile. There was no way Phoenix could get close enough to either use Blódbál's power or to apply any aikido techniques.

Wait! Aikido – that was it. Direct confrontation was not the answer. Redirection, not just of movement but of thought, that was the key. Time to turn the tables on this dude. Good thing he'd taken acting classes as a kid.

Staggering again, Phoenix let out a groan. Dropping Blódbál from apparently-nerveless fingers, he fell to his knees in the dust and hung his head as though defeated. Dimly, he heard Cadoc's triumphant cry and the excited babble of new voices. The sound of steel-on-steel told him help must have come for the others, in some form. Head down, Phoenix waited for his chance.

With a deep chuckle, his foe swung his sword, ready to deliver a death-blow. Phoenix tensed, heart pounding, watching from the corners of his eyes. This could go horribly wrong if he wasn't fast enough. Sweat prickled on his forehead. His fingers itched to snatch Blódbál safely back into his hand.

He had to wait.

The Indian ran forward, sweeping his blade over and down to slice through the exposed back of Phoenix's neck. At the last possible second, Phoenix spun on one knee, moving closer - directly *into* the man's knees. He dropped low and jammed his shoulder into a leg. There was a sickening *snap* as one of the assassin's knees bent in completely the wrong direction. With a surprised cry of pain, he sailed awkwardly over Phoenix's back and landed heavily on the packed earth. His sword flew from a lax hand.

Swiftly, Phoenix seized Blódbál and held it to the bare throat.

"Who are you? Who sent you?" he demanded, panting. "What do you want?"

The man suppressed a groan of pain and bared his teeth. "I am Yajat. I follow the Han Emperor's DragonMaster. He ordered the white woman's death. We have fulfilled our task. Do what you wish with me. My master will be pleased."

"The DragonMas…oh." Phoenix shook his head. "Zhudai again, huh? Well you can go back to your master and tell him he's wasting his time. We *will*…no, better yet, just tell him to put the kettle on, since we'll be dropping in for tea one of these days, soon."

Grinning at the bemused look in the man's eyes, Phoenix moved Blódbál a few centimetres away. He jerked his head toward the edge of camp.

"Go on. Get out of here. Go back and tell him."

The Indian stared at him in shock then gritted his teeth and pushed himself upright. His right lower leg dangled uselessly at an odd angle. He gasped in pain as the toe touched the earth.

Phoenix screwed up his nose, keeping Blódbál hovering inches from the man's throat.

"Sorry about that. Maybe your master can fix it. Don't like your chances, though. He didn't strike me as the compassionate sort."

The Indian picked up his sword and began to hobble painfully away, casting venomous looks over his shoulder as he did. Phoenix re-sheathed Blódbál and watched him for awhile before turning back to check on his friends.

"You ok?" Cadoc approached, a strange expression on his face as he eyed the retreating assassin.

Behind him, Marcus cradled Jade's limp form and began to carry her toward their tent. Brynn hovered, looking none the worse for wear. Vasi and a team of his men despatched the few remaining assassins who dared to test their strength. The ground was littered with dead and dying, black-clad swordsmen.

"Sure." Phoenix shrugged.

The action reminded him that he really wasn't that 'ok'. His back was on fire and his face stung. Jade would be out of action for awhile, so he'd have to get some doctoring from one of the local shamans. Scary.

Vasi approached, concern mingling with respect and regret on his handsome face. "The Devi Jade," he asked, "is she alright?"

Phoenix translated for Cadoc and exchanged a knowing look. "She'll be ok," he assured the Indian prince. "It looked worse than it is, I'm sure."

"What about you?" The prince walked around, inspecting the sluggishly-bleeding wound on Phoenix's back. "You need to see a surgeon. Who sent these men?" He frowned down at the bodies.

Phoenix shrugged again, regretting it. "No idea," he lied. "One of them called himself Yajat and had a freaky, long, flexible sword, though."

Vasi's eyes widened. "An urumi! They are a difficult weapon to master and an even harder one to defeat in the hands of one who has. The assassin Yajat is known far and wide. If you have bested him then you are a hero indeed. Where is he now?" He looked again at the pile of dead bodies.

"I broke his knee and let him go with a warning to his master." Phoenix waved a hand in the direction the assassin had taken. There was nothing but darkness now.

The Indian prince paled. "You defeated Yajat, the best Kalaripayattu assassin, and let him go? Are you insane?"

Phoenix groaned. "Probably. Was that a dumb thing to do?"

"Only if you like living," Vasi replied. "You have dishonoured him and he *will* seek vengeance."

"Oh good," Phoenix sighed. "Someone else out to get me. How unusual. C'mon, let's go see how Jade is."

Vasi opened his mouth to argue then seemed to think better of it. He blinked a few times, raised his brows and shook his head in apparent astonishment. Clearly he wasn't used to someone dismissing such danger so lightly. Phoenix chuckled, remembering the almost-constant state of adrenalin-rush he'd been in when he'd first arrived in this ancient time. Now, living with the threat of death seemed almost normal. It made his real life seem extremely dull by comparison and his previous fear of his stepfather almost laughable. What were a few threats compared to being skewered, poisoned, shot and squashed? Maybe things would change a little when he got home…

Phoenix shook himself. *If* he got home. He couldn't afford to get complacent now. Jade had probably lost another life, which left her with only, what, four? They hadn't yet completed this level and still had the last to go. She couldn't risk losing any more and he couldn't afford to become blasé about his own.

Together, the three made their way to where Marcus had taken Jade. Cadoc went in. Outside the tent, Phoenix paused and looked at Vasi.

"Er… thanks for your help back there but maybe you shouldn't come in," he said.

"My father will wish to know the *devi* is indeed alright." Vasi's tone brooked no argument. "Our success in the forthcoming battle depends on her."

Phoenix hesitated, wondering if Jade had had time to recover; wondering how many lives she'd lost. As he did, the tent flap flipped aside and Brynn stepped out, looking relieved and cheerful again. He took it as a good sign. Brynn tended to get upset when Jade died. Cadoc came out. Marcus emerged a second later, looking troubled.

"Is she alright?" Phoenix squeezed the boy's shoulder. He spoke in Breton and rolled his eyes significantly toward Vasi.

Brynn glanced that way then nodded, replying in Sanskrit so Vasi could understand. "Cadoc gave her some wine and that seemed to help. She's just changing into her own clothes – that sari was pretty mangled. Basically, she's pretty annoyed but she'll be fine." He switched to Svear. "She protected the Bag, though."

"Is she annoyed because of what happened, or because her sari got wrecked," Phoenix asked in Sanskrit.

"Er…" Brynn considered it, "both, I think. Who did it, anyway?"

Phoenix grimaced and switched languages again. "Our old friend, Zhudai. He's now calling himself 'DragonMaster' and has hired some new friends."

"Oh good," Marcus sighed, "we needed more of those sorts of friends."

Phoenix quirked him a lopsided grin. "I do believe that was sarcasm. Didn't know you had it in you."

"I save it for special occasions," the Roman retorted. "She lost one more, you know." He eyed Phoenix's life-dagger.

"I'd guessed as much," he returned. Turning to Vasi and ignoring his puzzled frown, Phoenix smiled a polite dismissal. "Looks like the fun's over for the evening. We'll stick with Jade and make sure she gets rest. See you in the morning."

Vasi hesitated, obviously reluctant to go without seeing Jade for himself.

At that moment, Brynn let out a squeak of delight and pointed toward the sky. "Look, shooting stars – lots of them."

Everyone looked up. Sure enough, dozens of shooting stars arced across the night sky in a spectacular light-show display.

Marcus laid a hand on Phoenix's shoulder. "I don't think-" he began.

At the same time, Vasi gasped and Cadoc murmured, "Uh-oh, looks like you were wrong about the fun being over. I think it's just starting."

CHAPTER FOURTEEN

Seconds later, the first fire-arrow hit a tent nearby and flames ate their way up the canvas wall. Someone inside screamed. Five half-dressed men ran out, yelling and pointing. More arrows rained down. More blazes erupted. Fires blossomed all over the camp, sending sparks high into the air. Horses whinnied in fear and elephants trumpeted their distress. More voices joined the cacophony until everything was a babble of noise and confusion. Acrid smoke poured into the dark sky, blotting out the stars.

"Marcus, get Jade and our things out of there. Fast," Phoenix ordered. "I'll go find the horses. Brynn, you're with me. Cadoc, help Marcus."

Marcus nodded. He and Cadoc plunged back into the tent.

Vasi collared a nearby officer and issued rapidfire orders.

"Know where they're keeping the horses, Brynn?" Phoenix scanned the darkness, watching.

"You're kidding, aren't you?" the boy said. "Of course I know. I also know where they store the water. We can get some buckets and start people putting out the fires."

"No." Phoenix grabbed his arm just as the boy turned to dash off. "That's what they're expecting. Help me get the horses, Jade and our gear to safety then we need to arrange a defence."

"That's what *who* will be expecting."

"Probably Bhumaka's men." Phoenix had a feeling this was going to be a long night. "They obviously don't have the same problem with using guerrilla warfare that Marcus does. If I were them, I'd be positioning for an attack about now – to take the camp while it's in chaos."

Vasi appeared at his elbow. "I need to get the men organised to put out these fires. Will you help me?"

Phoenix shook his head and repeated his theory. "I think the fires are the least of your worries. You need to be mustering a defence. This is the prelude to an assault."

The prince stared at him in disbelief. "An assault? In the middle of the night? Surely even Bhumaka is not so dishonourable as that?"

Phoenix raised an eyebrow at him. "What's honourable to one man is stupidity to another, your highness. It's up to you but I'm not wasting my time on fires. If you decide to organise protection, let me know." Turning on his heel, he followed Brynn into the smoky darkness. Behind, Vasi wavered for a moment then growled and ran off, presumably to report to his father.

The horses were close by. Corralled with several cavalry animals, they were bunched up in one corner of the pen; eyes rolling and heads tossing in fear as flames jumped high around them.

Brynn found their tack and together they managed to get all six of their remaining beasts saddled and bridled. Phoenix tried to ignore the burning pains in his back and face as the cuts there pulled wider each time he moved. Healing would have to wait.

Riding back through camp was faster but fraught with danger. Scared soldiers and panicked servants dashed in all directions, achieving little but adding to the general chaos. The wind picked up and black smoke swirled in strange eddies between the tents. Phoenix tied a strip of cloth over his nose and mouth in an attempt to keep it out. His eyes watered.

In the distance, he heard the sound of war-trumpets but there was no way of knowing whose side was called to arms. If Vasi had not taken his advice, this could be a very short, very brutal battle.

They reached the tent just as a flaming projectile smacked into the bottom edge of one wall and fire began licking its way up the side. Marcus and Cadoc emerged, laden with packs and gear. Jade followed, looking ghastly. She was pale and still smeared with streaks of her own blood. She stumbled and clung onto the tentrope, coughing as smoke swirled around them.

Phoenix swung down and helped her to her horse. She seemed to lack the strength to even haul herself into the saddle, so he half-lifted her. She gathered the reins and gave him a wan smile.

"You ok?" He asked anxiously.

She nodded. "I won't be much help in this, though," she admitted, waving a hand at the destruction being wrought around them. "I need time and rest. I've lost too much blood and strength to perform any major magic."

Phoenix gripped her leg. "I figured as much. Leave this to us. You and Brynn get out of here. Cadoc!" he yelled over at the other Player. "Find them a safe place to hide nearby, will you?"

The Player nodded and slumped in his saddle, leaving his digital body behind while he searched Google Maps for a hiding place. Moments later, he straightened.

"Ride north-north-east for about a kilometre and you should find three low hills," he said to Jade. "The middle one has a narrow ridge up the western side with a path on it. There's no trees but you should be safe up there. It'll be easily defensible and you'll have a great view," he added with a smile. "Good luck."

Jade laid a hand on his arm. "You too. All of you. Be careful, Phoenix."

Phoenix nodded then frowned at Brynn when the boy looked mulish. "Just go, please Brynn," he pleaded. "I know you want to stay but we can't leave Jade alone when she's so weak. Please?"

Sighing, the boy nodded, scrambled ungracefully aboard his pony and gathered up the reins. He looked back several times.

Phoenix watched them vanish into the gloom and wondered if he'd done the right thing. Jade was in no state to help and if she stayed, he and Marcus would spend their whole time protecting her.

Cadoc nudged his horse closer. "You do realise we all could have gone, don't you?"

Phoenix blinked at him in shock. It had never occurred to him to run away. "We made a deal with Guatamiputra. We promised to help him win this war."

The Player shrugged. "I just don't see how this is going to help you finish your Quest, that's all. Hard to win if you're dead."

"Maybe it's not just about winning," Phoenix muttered defensively.

Cadoc laughed. "You really are nuts. What else would it be about?" He didn't stay to hear an answer but kneed his horse into a trot and headed off toward the Raj's tent. Around him, smoke and flame swirled.

Marcus came alongside, controlling his nervous horse with an iron hand. "You're right, he's not."

"Thanks." Phoenix wasn't so sure. It was nice to hear but he could see Cadoc's point, too. From the outsiders' viewpoint, Phoenix's choice would seem insane. There was nothing to be gained from staying and fighting someone else's war.

Then Jade's words from the previous level came to mind and Phoenix wavered again. She had made him realise that every decision they made could have either positive or negative results. In Svealand, they had opted to help innocent villagers and had won a shortcut to Asgard and the end of their quest. Something similar had happened when Brynn had convinced them to go treasure-hunting in Egypt. For Phoenix and Jade, there were no clear-cut paths through this game. Like real life, every decision had consequences – their path was the product of their choices, good and bad.

Phoenix shook himself. "Let's go find the Raj. We have a skirmish to win."

*****

Jade bent low over her mare's neck, clutching the mane with one hand and the reins of Cadoc's spare horse with the other. Ahead, Brynn cast anxious glances back at her as he picked a way through the frenzied camp. Twice men jumped out at them, intent on stealing the horses and escaping fiery death. The first time, Brynn landed a kick and the would-be thief fell back, unconscious. The second time, Jade's horse reared and this man backed away fearfully as she clung to the reins.

By the time they reached the northern edge of the camp, Jade's whole body shook with exhaustion and she could barely stay in the saddle. So when a third, dark-clad man leaped from the shadows and swung himself up onto the back of Cadoc's second horse, she was powerless to prevent it. He jerked the reins from her hands and flashed her a grin, his teeth white in a soot-blackened face. Turning, he kicked the animal into a gallop and vanished into the night, leaving Jade to thump her fist on her thigh in weak frustration.

"Cadoc's going to kill me," she moaned as Brynn came alongside.

"Not if I can help it." He glowered. "C'mon, we need to get to that hill before all hell breaks loose here. I hear fighting."

Jade strained to hear above the crackling of flames and cries for help. Sure enough, Brynn was right. Added to the general noise of confused fire-fighting was the sound of steel on steel. The battle had begun.

Together, they urged their horses into a canter, reluctant to go any faster on the uneven, nightshadowed terrain. Jade managed to whisper a few pathetic witchlights into existence and sent them to bob ahead, just above the ground. They rode more rapidly after that and it wasn't long before the horses were picking their way up the bare spine of the ridge Cadoc had found.

Sounds of warfare carried clearly through the cool night air and the scent of smoke stung their throats. The horses huffed and bobbed their heads as they struggled up the steep slope. Jade shivered with fatigue as she clung to her mare's mane. She barely remembered climbing the last few dozen metres to the top of the ridge. It was only when Brynn gasped at the view that she managed to sit up and take notice of what was happening.

Far below, Guatamiputra's camp was a shambles. By the uneven flickering of burning tents and supply depots, it was clear that Bhumaka's nighttime surprise campaign had devastated the army. How could the Raj possibly win, now? Where were her friends in that milling mass of frightened people and stampeding animals?

With an effort, Jade felt for the mental connection of the Binding Spell that linked her to Phoenix and Marcus. It focussed her vision so she could make out Phoenix alongside Vasi, Marcus and Cadoc, rallying troops into a rough fighting formation. In and out of the tents they wove, hacking and slicing their way through any of Bhumaka's men they found.

"What's happening?" Brynn asked, tugging on her sleeve.

Realising his vision wasn't as farsighted as hers, she gave him a running commentary.

"The guys are with Vasi. They're trying to organise enough troops to fight back. Guatamiputra and his generals are doing the same on the other side of the camp." She bit her lip. "But they can't see that Bhumaka's Saka troops are coming right up the middle between them. If they knew, they're in perfect position to squeeze them and end this now. Damn!"

Brynn was practically jumping up and down in his saddle. "Phoenix!" he yelled into the night. Helplessly, he turned back to her. "Can't you do *anything? We need to be able to tell them.*"

Jade chewed harder on her lip. She had very little strength at the moment but this could be a crucial turning point in the war. If Guatamiputra could wipe out a large portion of Bhumaka's elite troops now, the big battle would be easier to win. Brynn was right. She had to do something but what?

A thought niggled. What was it Marcus had said that afternoon when they were discussing battle tactics; something that was a problem for all armies but especially for big armies? Screwing up her face, Jade struggled to remember, regretting that she'd zoned out.

Of course! Communication. Exactly the problem she and Brynn were facing now. They could see everything but they couldn't relay it to anyone who mattered.

Or could they?

Galvanised, she sat up straight. "Get me my herb bag, some of that dried fruit and the wine-skin Heron gave us."

He gave her an incredulous look. "Is now the time for a picnic?"

She glared at him. "Just get them."

"Alright, alright." He fumbled in the gear-bags on his horse and handed her what she'd asked for. She stuffed a couple of handfuls of fruit into her mouth and washed it down with a mouthful of wine. It wasn't the rest and sleep she needed but it would give her enough energy to complete this task – hopefully.

Next she extracted a small ginseng root from her herb-bag. Ginseng was known even in the modern world as a good pick-me-up and she hoped it would do the same thing now. Taking a deep breath, she put it in her mouth and chewed, grimacing at its bitter, earthy taste.

Within seconds, she felt a flood of energy warming her chilled body. It was working. Touching her fingers to the yin-yang amulet at her neck, Jade felt power from it, too, pouring into her. Now she was ready. It might not last long, though, this artificial strength. She'd better make the most of it. Whispering *heili-tala*, she focussed her thoughts on Phoenix and spoke his name.

"Phoenix, can you hear me?"

There was a sense of startled recognition and a brief flicker of fear rapidly suppressed.

"It's ok," she whispered. *"Brynn and I are safe up on the mountain. We can see everything."*

"Jade?" His mental voice sounded muted and distant, like she heard him from the end of a long, echoey tunnel.

"Who else?" she said tartly. *"I can't keep this up for long so listen. Bhumaka's men have taken the middle of the camp. Guatamiputra is fighting on the western side, so if you can both turn inward, you'll have the Saka contingent trapped and you can win this."*

There was a pause and she sensed Phoenix struggling to fight and keep up this mind-talk at the same time. She waited impatiently for him to focus on it again. When he did, it was brief and to the point.

"Alright. You talk to Guatamiputra and tell him we'll both move in three minutes, no more." Abruptly, the sense of his presence ended, as though he'd hung up on her. Shocked, she jerked back and sought him with her eyes. Relief flowed as she saw him still fighting hard with Marcus right beside him.

Turning west, she found Guatamiputra and concentrated on him. It was more difficult because she didn't know him well and found him a bit intimidating.

How would he react to hearing her voice in his head? Maybe it was time to play the *devi* to the hilt.

Gritting her teeth, she threw her thoughts at him as strongly as she could.

"Raj, hear me. It is the Shining One. Obey my instructions and you can win this battle."

Far below, Guatamiputra's sword arm faltered in mid strike. Frightened, she yelled at him.

"Don't stop fighting, you idiot, or you'll be killed before you can even begin to unite your kingdom!"

The Raj completed his swing and despatched the man he'd been duelling with. Jade sagged in the saddle, relieved. Swiftly, she relayed instructions about the Saka to the king, hoping he would believe her.

Brynn tugged on her arm, pointing. Phoenix and Vasi were turning their men westward. If Guatamiputra didn't do his part, Vasi's men would be outnumbered and slaughtered.

With a mental and real cry that all but scraped her throat raw, Jade shouted at the Raj.

"Move you fool or Vasi, Phoenix and all their men will die now. Move!"

With that huge effort, the last of her temporary strength drained away and she lost the mental connection. Her fingers fell from the amulet. Vaguely, she felt Brynn's small hands trying to hold her up as she slid forward and plunged from her mare's neck to the cold, hard ground below.

CHAPTER FIFTEEN

The sound of hammering woke her. Muffled and regular, it drove into Jade's sleepy dreamstate and dragged her back into what passed for reality. Sighing regretfully, she raised sticky eyelids and stared at a canvas ceiling. Her limbs seemed too heavy to bother moving, so she stayed still, wondering where she was – and who the heck was into major construction somewhere nearby.

Turning her head, she saw familiar packs and gear strewn carelessly around the place. Four other sets of bedding seemed to indicate all her friends were alive and well and that this was not some sort of prison. So far, so good. Now for the real test. Was *she* alive and well, or just well-ish.

Cautiously, she sat up. It was surprisingly easy, considering how awful she'd felt the last couple of days. Maybe she'd slept long enough to regain some strength after being drugged by Leela and losing two lives in two days.

Memories of the battle rushed back and she patted the ground around her, looking for her life-dagger. It lay beside the wadded up pile of clothes that served as her pillow. Holding it gingerly, Jade counted the rubies in the hilt and groaned. There were only three left. Only three. That meant she'd lost yet another one by draining her strength on top of the mountain.

Anger surged and she gripped the hilt until her

knuckles turned white. It wasn't *fair*. Just doing that simple little bit of magic shouldn't have taken so much out of her. She wasn't some sort of pathetic weakling girly-girl. She was stronger than that. What was *wrong* with her? It just wasn't *fair*. With a cry of frustration, she flung the dagger impetuously away and fought the urge to burst into tears.

"Hey! Watch out! You could kill someone with that thing," Cadoc's voice called in mock alarm from the doorway. He stepped all the way in and added, "At least you could if I gave you some lessons. Knife-throwing is obviously not your strong point. I've been teaching Phoenix, though, and he's getting pretty good. How are you feeling?"

Jade looked up, managing a small smile and a shrug. He came in, bearing a steaming mug and followed by Brynn, Phoenix and Marcus. They crowded around, all talking at once about winning the battle, Guatamiputra's gratitude and something about onagers. Jade took the tea, warming her fingers on it and her heart on their friendship. Her smile broadened.

"Thanks guys," she said as their stories petered out and they looked expectantly at her. She raised her mug at Cadoc. "Thanks for the tea; and thanks for taking care of me, all of you. I'm sorry to be so useless at the moment. I don't know why I'm so tired these days." Turning her head she brushed a tear away with the back of her hand and sniffed defiantly.

Phoenix laid a hand on her shoulder and squeezed. "You aren't useless. You won the battle for us. I just hope you're feeling better now. You can't afford to lose any more lives like that."

She smiled. "Last night was an exception. Hopefully I won't have to do magic in such a weakened state again."

The others exchanged amused glances. "The camp was attacked *two* nights ago," Phoenix broke it to her.

"You've been asleep for a whole day, a night and most of today as well."

Jade stared at him then shook herself, trying to account for the lost time. "Well," she finally said matter-of-factly, "no wonder I'm bursting to go to the bathroom. Get out, you lot, give a girl some privacy." Waving a hand at them she shooed them away and clambered out of bed to get ready.

If she'd been asleep that long then they only had one more day before the last night of the dying moon. Tomorrow night they had to complete their quest. Tomorrow night they had to find the statue of Vishnu and return the Sudarshana or they wouldn't be able to get to Level Five.

The sound of renewed hammering roused her from fruitless worry about how to accomplish their task. She finished dressing, tucked the Hyllion Bagia into her shirt, the knife into her belt, picked up her staff and stepped outside. Blinking in the bright afternoon light, she stared at the enormous shapes silhouetted against the blue sky.

"They're huge," she said stupidly.

Phoenix, who'd been waiting with the others, grinned at her. "Marcus' idea come to life. After your stunt with the telepathy, Guatamiputra was more than willing to listen to Marcus' plan."

"Marcus' plan?" Jade repeated in disbelief.

"I know. Hard to believe, isn't it?" Phoenix grinned. "Even more bizarre is the fact that he talked non-stop for an hour, explaining how to use the onagers in battle. He's a born general, although he's quite irritated that the Indians don't seem to grasp the idea of using cavalry properly and he doesn't have enough time to teach them." He sent a sideways grin at the Roman, who ignored him and continued his low-voiced conversation with Vasi.

Phoenix leaned closer and murmured into Jade's ear. "Between you and me, Marcus is appalled at the waste of human life. Although the Raj is willing to listen to new ideas, his generals' idea of war is to throw a hundred thousand of the lower, *shudra* caste infantry at each other and count victory by how many are still standing at the end of the day. That's part of the reason Marcus had so much trouble convincing the generals that the onager are a good idea – they just couldn't imagine war without losing obscene numbers of men on both sides."

Jade opened her mouth to ask exactly what Marcus' plan was but was interrupted when Vasi finished his conversation with Marcus and came up to her. He bowed, open admiration in his dark eyes.

"If you are recovered, my lady, my father requests an audience."

She raised surprised brows at Phoenix, who shrugged. This was a turnabout. Last time Guatamiputra had barely tolerated her speaking to him; now he was requesting an audience? Intrigued, she followed the prince. Phoenix and the others fell into step like an honour guard.

Inside Guatamiputra's tent, the Raj was arguing heatedly with one of his advisors. He broke off when Jade arrived.

"Ah! You are recovered!" Nodding, the king gestured for them to sit.

His huge, wooden table had, presumably, been burnt so they crowded around a small, rickety contraption made out of wooden boxes covered with a sari. Jade hid a smile. How the mighty had fallen.

"What do you think of this idea; the way your Marcus wants to deploy this new machinery?" the Raj demanded loudly.

"Oh," she stalled. She had no clue what the whole plan was. "Well, why don't you tell me how you see it playing out then I'll tell you what I think of it."

Nothing loath, Guatamiputra explained Marcus' plan in enthusiastic detail.

His army had already retreated from their burnt-out campground and were now camped behind the very hill where Jade had fallen insensible. Bhumaka had, at first, waited to see what they would do. Now he was bringing men across the river to stake a claim on the abandoned site. Marcus had ordered a number of large onager to be built out of sight, just behind the crests of the three hills, with several more held in reserve on the flat land below. In addition, he taught the men how to construct pitch-coated balls of wickerwork that could be hurled from the onager as an alternative to rocks. The previous night, Guatamiputra's men had been busy digging shallow trenches all along the northern border of the old campsite and filling them with pitch and straw. Elephants were put to work hauling large rocks and baskets of gravel and sand from a nearby riverbed.

Now the Raj's entire army hid behind the three hills, with scouts keeping a lookout for any indication that Bhumaka was going to attack. So far, Bhumaka had contented himself with simply sweeping aside the remains of Guatamiputra's old encampment and setting up his own.

Guatamiputra shrugged. "Let him exhaust his men in pointless gestures. Tomorrow, at dawn, we will attack – but with just half our army."

Jade raised her brows at him then glanced at Marcus, who nodded in solemn confirmation.

"After the initial attack, we will turn and retreat toward these hills." Guatamiputra pointed at a rough model that sat on the rickety table.

She now realised that the upturned cups and bowls, and dozens of pebbles were not simply unwashed dishes and clutter but meant to represent hills and armies.

"That will keep our men out of range of their poisoned arrows. With your mind-talk, it will be easy to co-ordinate an attack and a unified retreat," Guatamiputra explained. "Bhumaka will think they have won and will chase after us.

When his army is close enough, we will launch the onager. Some will throw rocks and fire directly into the army and others will set fire to the trenches we dug – cutting off his retreat. The rest of the army will then sweep in from either side, lead by the war-chariots, and enclose Bhumaka's men, crushing them as though in a huge vice." He closed his hand together in a pincer movement. "You, my dear, will then soar above wielding the Sudarshana and we will crush them in one, mighty battle. The Saka Kshatrap will be driven out of Satvahana land forever." He smacked a fist into his palm. His generals nodded enthusiastically.

With an effort, Jade suppressed a smile at his dramatic speech. Instead, she nodded. "Sounds like a good plan but there are two problems I can see straight away. One: I don't have a thirty foot eagle to fly over the battlefield on and two: what about the Naga?"

From their guilty, stunned expressions, she assumed all of her companions had completely forgotten to mention the existence of the snake-people in Bhumaka's army. Brynn groaned. Cadoc grimaced. Guatamiputra stared at them all with confusion and a hint of anger.

"What are you talking about?" he demanded.

"We forgot about them," Phoenix admitted. "Bhumaka has made some sort of agreement with the Naga people. They will be fighting for him."

Guatamiputra sat down, suddenly seeming older. He passed a hand over his face. Behind him, Vasi frowned and took a half-step forward while Sopaniputra quickly smothered a fleeting expression of excitement.

"How many?" Vasi asked.

"We don't know." Phoenix shrugged. "Jade?"

She shook her head. "I didn't hear. Can you send in scouts?"

Vasi thought then shook his head, too. "Bhumaka's camp is too well-guarded for any of my men to slip in."

"What about any of your *boys,*" Brynn piped up. All

eyes turned to him. He gave a one-shouldered shrug. "Just seemed to me that a small boy who can understand all their languages might be a useful spy…"

Guatamiputra raised his head, stood up and eyed Phoenix. "He is your servant, what do you say?"

Phoenix grinned down at Brynn and laid a hand on the boy's thin shoulder. "Brynn is no-one's servant, sir. He's his own man and if he thinks he can do it, I believe in him. It's his choice."

Jade made a wordless noise of protest but Phoenix and Brynn both ignored her.

"Besides," Brynn said out of the side of his mouth in the Svear language, "if I get caught and put in prison again, I'm one up on you."

Phoenix grinned wider and squeezed his shoulder. "Do me a favour and don't."

"Jealous?"

"Hardly," Phoenix returned. "I just don't want to go to the hassle of having to rescue you again. It's getting to be such a drag."

Brynn elbowed him.

The Raj crouched down in front of the young Breton. "Very well, boy. Go tonight and return with as much information on Bhumaka's army as you can. It could mean the difference between success and failure tomorrow. You will be handsomely rewarded, I promise."

Brynn sent him a narrow look. "Exactly how handsome are we talking, your Raj-ness?"

Several generals gasped and a serving girl carrying a tray of food into the tent squeaked in alarm. For a moment, the Raj glared at the boy then his face softened into a cynical smile. He stood and laid a heavy hand on Brynn's shoulder.

"You haggle like a true Indian, boy. Let us say, as many of my gold coins as you can hold in two hands."

"The coins and two new horses," Brynn countered,

"since we lost two in helping you so far."

"The coins and *one* new horse," the Raj replied, dropping his hand and giving the boy a severe look. "You lost the first by your own carelessness."

Seeing he'd pushed the issue as far as he could, Brynn quirked a lopsided grin and gave the Raj a mock-salute. "It's a bargain, your highness. Back soon." Without another word, he spun and was gone from the tent.

Several hours later, even Marcus was edgy. Brynn had been away a very long time. It was well after dark. Guatamiputra had ordered the bulk of his army to bed in preparation for the next day. The night outside was broken only by the regular pacing of guards and the occasional trumpeting of an elephant or whickering of a horse.

Inside the Raj's tent, however, no one had left. The Raj, Vasi, Sopaniputra, the generals, Phoenix and his companions sat, fidgeted or paced as they awaited Brynn's return. Phoenix borrowed Cadoc's knives and went outside to practice his new knife-throwing skill for awhile. Marcus polished and sharpened all their weapons with single-minded focus. Jade curled up in a corner, succumbing again to sleep as her weary body tried to recover.

Eventually, servants brought food, which was eaten in subdued silence then taken away again. Any new conversations quickly stumbled to a halt in the oppressive atmosphere. Marcus and Vasi continued to come up with variations on the war plan in an effort to pass the time. Cadoc hovered solicitously around Jade, bringing her food, drink and her cloak when the temperatures fell. Sopaniputra glared alternately at him and at his father, as though angry at both for some reason.

Jade managed to stay calm. Since the Binding Spell attached the four companions in a way she could sense, she could at least tell Brynn was not injured in any way. It was still taking far too long, though.

Finally, just as she had decided she couldn't stand

waiting any longer, the tent flap burst open and Brynn staggered in, breathing hard.

"Are you alright?" She rushed to his side, running her hands over his head and face to check he really was ok.

He brushed her aside with a nod. "I'm fine. I'm fine."

"Give the boy some space," Guatamiputra ordered.

He pressed a glass of warm wine into Brynn's hands and waited impatiently while he gulped it down. Someone handed the Breton boy a chapatti and he bit into it. Washing it down with more wine, he sighed and sat on a stool.

"From what I can tell, those Saka troops you fought the other night weren't Saka at all," he began, his mouth still half-full. Waving away astonished interruptions, Brynn shouted to make himself heard. "It was all part of the trick. They dressed up a bunch of ordinary Indian infantry and sent them in to take the brunt of your defence. The idea was to make you believe you'd taken out the best of Bhumaka's men so you'd over commit yourself in the main battle."

A babble of angry, confused conversation broke out amongst the generals as they argued over the honour of Bhumaka's tactics. Sopaniputra loudly advised his father to give up and return east to defend his capital. Phoenix looked at Brynn, as though sensing there was more to come. Guatamiputra hushed his advisors and motioned for the boy to continue.

"What about the Naga?" he asked.

"Ah." Brynn scrubbed his fingers through his hair, sending a shower of dust up into the air around him. "The Naga. I couldn't get too close, you understand, because they would know my scent – from when we saw some in Bhumaka's camp," he added, catching Jade's warning look. The last thing they needed was for Guatamiputra to find out exactly who was responsible for the Naga taking sides in this war.

"Yes, yes." The Raj made 'hurry up' motions with his hands.

"There would have to be at least ten thousand Naga warriors in Bhumaka's army," Brynn finished in a rush.

Guatamiputra sat down heavily. His generals exchanged anxious looks. Sopaniputra muttered again something about retreating. Vasi and Marcus both frowned, glancing at the table with its rough-and-ready model of the two armies. Clearly they were re-thinking their battle strategy.

"Umm," Brynn added with apparent reluctance. "There's something else you might not like."

The Raj sighed. "Go on, boy. You may as well tell us. It can't get much worse."

"I'm not so sure about that," the boy warned. "The Naga goddess, Manasa, is with them and she sounds really, really angry."

CHAPTER SIXTEEN

Phoenix looked over quickly at Jade. She paled, clutching her chair with white fingers.

"How?" Her voice was low and strained.

If Guatamiputra thought it was an odd question, he didn't say so. He simply nodded slowly and stood up.

"Rumours had reached us that Manasa devi had been killed in a fight with a treasure-hunter," he mused. "Clearly she either wasn't killed or she has simply taken a new avatar. Either way, she is a force to be reckoned with and one we must factor into our plans. Luckily, we have our own *devi*." He bowed toward Jade, who stared back with wide, horror-filled eyes.

"Come gentlemen," the Raj continued more confidently, "we have plans and preparations to make. This is a setback but nothing we can't handle."

Phoenix, however, was watching Jade. She put her hand to her head and stood up, holding onto the back of a chair as though afraid she would fall over if she let go. Cadoc was quickly by her side, one hand under her elbow. She smiled up at him.

"I don't feel so well," she apologised. "I think I'll go to bed."

Phoenix nodded and caught Brynn's eye. The boy lifted his chin in silent understanding.

"Me too," he yawned. "I'll come with you."

Together, the two left the tent.

Marcus moved over to Phoenix's side and murmured into his ear. "She doesn't look any better, does she?"

Phoenix shook his head. "I don't know if it's just the thought of dealing with that snake-goddess again, or whether it's the after-effects of so many deaths but I'm worried about her. This weakness is not normal. We need her in full strength tomorrow if we're going to utilise her telepathy to keep the army co-ordinated. Then there's this whole eagle-and-sudarshana thing. Where and when does that factor in? There's still too much we don't know." He ran stiff fingers through his hair and growled low in his throat.

"If it's any consolation, fire should work just as well on the Naga as it does on human soldiers," Marcus said calmly. "If we aim well, we should also be able to cause their elephants to stampede into their own ranks."

Phoenix gripped his friend's arm, trying to convey his gratitude. "You've done an amazing job with this, Marcus. Thanks. I wouldn't have known where to start in managing a whole army."

The Roman boy bowed, his face flushed. He clearly wasn't used to receiving compliments; just as Phoenix wasn't used to giving them. Overcoming the awkward moment, Marcus turned his back on the rest of the tent-group and switched to the Svear language.

"Don't forget, too, that tomorrow night is the last night we'll see the moon. Whatever else happens, we have to return the Sudarshana to the statue of Vishnu in Punya-Vishaya by then. If we haven't won the war, the town will still be in Bhumaka's hands."

"I know!" Phoenix groaned. "I just don't know what to do. Damn, why did Jade have to pick now to get sick?"

"I'm pretty sure she didn't plan it," Marcus said levelly.

Phoenix smiled. "More sarcasm? Be careful or I'll start to think you have a sense of humour."

"Never," the Roman boy returned. One of the generals claimed his attention and Phoenix was left to ponder his own thoughts.

He had come to depend on Jade over the last couple of weeks. It had been unwilling in the beginning but their adventures led him to realise that she was someone he *could* rely on. Sure, she was a know-it-all who was too soft-hearted for her own good but she was smart and quick-thinking. Between the two of them, they covered each others' weaknesses. His fighting skills were complemented by her magic; her tendency to worry tempered his impulsive confidence. The realisation dawned on him that, in fact, they balanced each other quite nicely.

Phoenix slapped his own forehead and plonked down on a chair. "Of course we do. How stupid am I?" He murmured to himself. "This has been about balance all along. Each quest restores balance to the place we're in and there are two of us as Players because we *are* the yin and yang."

Reaching into his shirt, he fingered the half-amulet hanging around his neck. A muted surge of something that felt like strength and pride flowed into him via his fingertips. Startled, he dropped the pendant and squinted down at it. It had never done *that* before. Cautiously, he touched it again but this time it was just slightly warm, as normal.

With a shrug, he dismissed it and went to join in the planning meeting

*****

It was still dark when Jade awoke to the sound of someone calling her name softly. Blinking bleary eyes, she saw Marcus crouched nearby, holding a small oil lamp.

"What?" she croaked.

"It's time to get up," he said. He smiled at her and brushed a loose lock of hair from her face with gentle fingers.

"Why?" she asked, feeling thick-headed.

His expression slid into grim intent. "We go to war today."

That woke her up. A quick glance showed Phoenix and Cadoc already gone, along with their weapons and riding gear. Brynn still slept, curled up in a small ball of twitching legs and arms.

"You should have woken me earlier," she grouched, scrambling to her feet.

She'd gone to bed already-dressed, so it was just a matter of pulling on boots and grabbing her backpack. Marcus roused a sleepy, protesting Brynn.

"You needed the sleep," Marcus replied, shoving Brynn's things at him. "Let's go. We need to get to the top of the hill well before the dawn attack is launched. Guatamiputra will need your mind-speech as soon as it's light enough to see the battle."

Hurriedly, Jade grabbed her herb-bag and stuffed it, along with the Hyllion Bagia, into her shirt-front. She was going to need it. Her legs were shaky and her hands felt cold. There was a frightening core of weakness underlying the layer of strength that extra sleep had returned. Something was very wrong and she felt the first real twinges of fear: fear that she might collapse again, lose another life and lose the war, the level and the very game they were playing. Fear that she might never get home. Snatching up her staff, she leaned on it a little to disguise the trembling of her knees. Gritting her teeth, she nodded.

"Let's go then."

Marcus sent her a warm look, tinged with worry. "Don't lose any more lives doing this for the Raj," he ordered. "You are worth far more than him."

Jade slipped a hand through his arm and leaned her cheek on his strong shoulder. "Thanks, Marcus. Sometimes I have trouble believing that."

"I know," he replied, laying his hand over hers.

She smiled up at him. He frowned at her for a moment then leaned down and kissed her on the forehead.

"Be safe." Releasing her, he strode to his horse, leaving Jade to blink after him in surprise at his gruff tone.

A short while later, their sturdy horses carried them to the bare top of the same hill on which she and Brynn had sought refuge three nights before. Leaving Jade with the Raj, Brynn and one of the generals, Marcus hurried off to supervise the loading and aiming of the onagers.

Although it was too dark to see them yet, she knew there were twenty of the huge, wheeled contraptions lining the ridge and another twenty on each of the two mountains to the east and west of theirs. At the moment, they were hidden from the enemy but soon they would be pushed forward and loaded with enormous fireballs and rocks. Then death would rain down on Bhumaka's unsuspecting army.

Jade shivered at the thought. She could almost hear the screams.

The Raj gestured her closer. "You are well?" His sharp gaze bored into her. Dark circles under his eyes paid testimony to another sleepless night.

Unable to speak, Jade simply nodded. The knowledge that the responsibility of his war-communications rested on her shoulders weighed on her. What if she couldn't handle it? What if she failed? What if she wore herself out again at a crucial moment and the whole war went against Guatamiputra because he'd relied on her and she'd let him down? She struggled to control her spiralling fears.

Brynn sidled over, slipping his cold little hand into hers he looked up at her. "You'll be ok," he whispered, squeezing hard. Grateful, she squeezed back.

"Where are Phoenix and Cadoc?" she asked, trying to think of something else.

"They're with Vasi, leading the dawn attack," Brynn's answer was subdued. "They wouldn't let me go with them."

Jade squeezed his hand again. "I'm so glad they didn't, Brynn. I don't think I can do this without you."

The boy smiled up at her, his usual cheekiness swept away by the enormity of what they were taking part in.

"You can do anything," he said simply.

"I hope so," she said, under her breath.

The first faint hints of grey smudged the eastern horizon and Guatamiputra called her to his side. Together, she and Brynn crept to the southern edge of the mountain ridge and gazed down. Light blushed across the dark sky and spilled toward them over the vast Deccan Plateau below. One by one, the stars dimmed and were washed away by the dawn of a new day.

Bhumaka's camp could be seen faintly through the half-light and Jade was stunned at the extent of it. Tens of thousands of tents and smoking fires dotted the vast plains below. Thousands of elephants and horses shifted and stirred in safely corralled herds.

She could also just make out the forces of the Raj's army being lead by her friends. They lay and crouched in every scrap of cover; every gully; every shred of grass between the base of the hill and the encampment. They waited: waited for her signal to go to their deaths.

Guatamiputra nodded at her. She shivered and reluctantly sat crosslegged on a pile of cushions provided by someone thoughtful, and closed her eyes. Yesterday, while they were waiting for Brynn to return, she had discovered a limitation to her telepathy: she could only mind-speak people she'd met. Guatamiputra had ordered every one of his captains and commanders to attend him. Thousands of men had turned up.

Deeply embarrassed by the Raj's glowing introduction of her as a goddess, Jade brushed her thoughts delicately against theirs so she would know them and be able to find them again. It had been a trying, bizarre experience for everyone involved and now the whole army buzzed with rumours about her. While the spell lasted, Jade could hear the faint mind-whispers of all the men like a background hum in her head. It was distracting and, sometimes, distressing. It seemed the entire army was in awe of both her beauty and her power. Wild rumours of her abilities got wilder by the minute.

Now, almost unwillingly, she whispered the mind-talk spell and sought first for Phoenix. His mind was full of a muted battle-song. Blódbál's hymn, she guessed, only now realising how difficult he must find it to concentrate on anything else. In the back of her own mind, she could once more hear the low-key hum of Indian officers' thoughts. She blocked them out and focussed on Phoenix. Blódbál's battle-chant got louder.

"Ready?" she asked.

"As we'll ever be," Phoenix thought back.

En masse, she asked the same question of the commanders and of Marcus. They all replied affirmative, although in many she could sense awe and fear of her, mixed with fear of what lay ahead and worry for the men they commanded and their families. With a sigh, she opened her eyes and nodded to Guatamiputra. He glanced at the sky. It was now just light enough him to see clearly. His army crept as close as they could to the enemy camp and were in position.

It was now or never.

His fists clenched against the knowledge that many of his people were about to die and Jade respected him for that. In the last day or so, she had learnt a great deal about his family and it was clear they would be fine rulers. His family were of the Brahmin caste – priests and scholars, not warriors. Their rule had been just and fair for many years. Guatamiputra himself didn't want to go to war. He did it to regain lost Satavahana lands and to protect his people from the harsh governance of the Saka Kshatraps.

"Tell them to charge," the Raj commanded.

Helping Guatamiputra was the right thing to do. Keeping this firmly in mind, Jade reached out to all the officers at once and gave the order to go to war.

The feedback surge of excitement, fear, determination and adrenalin was so strong that she had to physically brace herself against it. She dampened the intensity of the connection to cope with the onslaught of emotion. Her heart raced and she had to take several deep breaths to focus again on her task: giving Guatamiputra a running commentary.

Far below, wild war-cries of sixty-thousand men rent the peaceful, grey dawn.

*****

Phoenix crouched in a shallow gully with his contingent of five hundred men and waited. A hundred metres away to the east, lying low in a similar wadi, Cadoc lay in wait with Sopaniputra and his men. Marcus had given them both a crash course on leading and co-ordinating a group this size but Phoenix's palms sweated at the thought of it.

To make matters worse, Blódbál seemed to sense the imminent slaughter and did its best to encourage him to run screaming into battle right now. He spoke firmly to the weapon. The song in his head paused in surprise. When it resumed it was fainter and carried a resentful overtone – like a child that continues rebelliously humming under its breath even after being asked to stop. Ah well; it was better, so he didn't push the point. At least he could hear Jade when she contacted him.

It was still a shock when her voice sounded inside his head. Would he ever get used to that? Could she hear any of his thoughts, or just the ones he spoke to her? It was an uncomfortable feeling and he knew her well. He wondered how the Indians were reacting to having her in their heads. From the startled, uneasy looks on some of his captains' faces, he guessed they weren't all that happy about it.

Dawn melted the darkness into a soft pink-grey and his group pressed themselves flat to the ground. They were hidden within a few dozen metres of the nearest Saka guard. This could all go pear-shaped if they were discovered early. With only a half-strength force, and without the elephants or war-chariots, the Raj's men would have to fight well and carefully to survive long enough to retreat at the right time.

Daylight crept across the plains, stealing night away and rousing sleepy birds. Behind him, Phoenix felt his men grow restless. Looking back, he glared at his officers, who, in turn, glared at their subordinates until the troops all settled again. So still were they, that a small brown bird came and sat on a branch only two feet from Phoenix's head and trilled its morning song, oblivious to the danger. He smiled. If that didn't convince Bhumaka's scouts that everything was fine, nothing would.

Tension built, doubled and redoubled as they waited for the call to battle. What seemed like an hour could only have been a few minutes, really. Phoenix willed himself to relax and let his fingers unclench from their cramped grip on Blódbál's hilt. He reviewed the battle plan again: sixty thousand of Guatamiputra's infantry would charge at Bhumaka's unwary camp as soon as it was light enough for the Raj to see everything. They would fight just long enough for the whole of Bhumaka's army to get into battle readiness. Then they would retreat as though being forced back. They would give ground until they were within range of the onager.

Then, on a prearranged signal, the Raj's troops would turn as one and bolt, leaving the bulk of Bhumaka's army within range of the catapults. Marcus would rain fire on to the enemy who would, hopefully, mill about in confusion for awhile and give time for Gautamputra's army to form up in full strength.

Finally, when fire and rocks had done their worst, the Raj would signal his whole army to descend on the demoralised enemy and finish the thing. Sixty thousand men would swarm out from behind the plains toward the centre, while two groups of thirty thousand swept around from the east and west in an attempt to outflank what remained of Bhumaka's force.

At least… That was the plan. Whether it worked or not would depend almost entirely on Jade's ability to keep communication lines open – and *that* depended on so many variables that it made Phoenix sick to even think of how many could go wrong.

His stomach churned as he was swept by the feeling that he was in the wrong place at the wrong time. What the heck was he doing here? Cadoc was right – it was stupid to fight someone else's war. He was going to die – again – and it would be a completely wasted life. How dumb was he? He didn't know how to lead this many men. He couldn't handle this.

Drawing a deep breath to steady his racing heart, he recalled Marcus' words in the Naga tunnels: *Only a fool ignores fear. Of course I get scared. I just don't let it paralyse me.* It was true: it was ok to be afraid; he just couldn't let it take over.

Then, as if aware of his thoughts, Blódbál's song burst forth in his head, wiping out all apprehension with battle-lust and images of glory. Phoenix pushed aside fear and grinned savagely. He *could* do it. Not so long ago, he'd been a kid afraid of his stepfather. Now he had fought battles on three continents and survived. The only difference here was the scale of things. With Blódbál in his hand and Jade backing him, he *could* do this.

Precisely at that moment, Jade's hollow voice sounded in his, and every other officers', head.

The order rang out. Phoenix waved his men forward. All around him, wild war-cries of sixty-thousand men rent

the peaceful, grey dawn.
The battle began.

CHAPTER SEVENTEEN

Phoenix leapt from his hiding place, closely followed by his battle contingent. Together, they merged with other bands. A thundering, roaring mass of men charged toward the northern edges of Bhumaka's camp. The sound of sixty-thousand male voices screaming abuse and sixty thousand pairs of feet thudding on the dry ground was awe-inspiring. A forest of swords, spears and knives of all description waved toward the brightening sky. Swarms of arrows darkened it again as archers rose to their feet to shoot over the heads of their own men and into Bhumaka's camp.

Since the idea wasn't to engage the whole enemy army, they were under orders to stick to the northern border of the camp. They were to make enough noise to rouse all the soldiers to combat. Accordingly, when Phoenix heard Jade's command in his head, he, along with all the other commanders, slowed their charge and looked for someone to fight.

They didn't have long to wait. Half-dressed and bleary-eyed, soldiers came pouring out of their tents and raced toward the fray. The first clash of steel rang out in the clear morning. Soon there were skirmishes up and down the line. Phoenix sent an anxious glance along the front row of his men. They held firm; faces purposeful and grim.

More and more of Bhumaka's men appeared. He was

too busy to spare more than the occasional glance around. A wave of Saka soldiers raced toward him – real ones this time. Their long coats flapped and their pointed hats marked them out amongst the shorter, less well-armed Indian natives. Bristling with weapons, they no longer reminded him of overgrown garden gnomes.

Grimly, Phoenix engaged them. Blood sprayed as Blódbál bit into the throat of a Saka warrior. Leaping the body, he blocked, spun, crouched and slashed at an exposed stomach. With a burbling gasp that was lost in the din, the soldier clutched at his belly and sank to his knees, mouth open in shock. Another took his place. Phoenix caught a fierce overhead blow on his new shield. The force of it numbed his arm and split the thin wood down the middle. He tossed the shield aside and ran the man through as he raised his arms to strike again.

With tingling fingers, Phoenix snatched out his dagger ploughed forward. Dimly, he heard Jade tell him that the men to his left were being pushed back and needed reinforcements. Without wasting the energy on acknowledging her, he yelled a command to his officers and the struggling group were propped up by fresher men.

Screams of the dying and the clash of steel-on-steel rang a harsh cacophony of death in the still morning air. They were echoed by the trumpeting of war elephants brought up from behind by Bhumaka's men. The earth shook with the thunder of their feet.

Around Phoenix, his men fell but they took an equal number of Bhumaka's men with them. The ground steamed and grew slippery with hot blood. Phoenix fought on, blocking his ears to the cries for help and his nose to the scent of fear, sweat, urine and blood. If he thought about what he did; about the carnage he took part in, he was afraid he'd throw up. Instead, he concentrated on Jade's faint commentary in his head. Blódbál's song made a glorious, dramatic background to her strained words.

Guatamiputra's men held.

It was almost time to retreat before the bulk of Bhumaka's army overwhelmed them.

Even as he thought it, the order to retreat rang in is head.

He moved back, still fighting as he went. Around him, his officers bellowed their orders and Guatamiputra's army began stage two of Marcus' grand plan.

Just as Phoenix began to think things might actually work, tall, a grim-eyed Indian warrior leapt forward, scanning the battlefield. Unarmoured, his dark, silken clothing fluttered as he jumped nimbly over his fallen comrades. Behind him slithered fifty or more Naga snake-people. One of them slid forward and spoke into the Indian's ear. The man's dark eyes fixed onto Phoenix and he nodded. He looked very familiar, for some reason. Memory surged in. Cursing, he called silently to Jade.

"Tell everyone the fangs are out in force. I've been spotted. That Indian from Bhumaka's tent is with them."

There was a brief, stricken silence from her, followed by a curt acknowledgement. All around him, his officers lifted their heads to see the new enemy as her warning reached them. He had no time to wonder if his men would break at the sight of the Naga. Their Indian leader wielded a long, curved sword with frightening skill; even hacking his way through his own men as he moved purposefully toward Phoenix.

Phoenix turned aside the first strike with Blódbál. He spun away as a Naga sliced through where he'd been standing. One swift blow despatched the snake-man before the Indian had time to get close again. Then the Indian leapt forward, slashing a furious flurry of blows at Phoenix's head, forcing him backward over the uneven ground. Even with Blódbál's magic to aid his skill, Phoenix was barely able to fend them off.

Confused, he skipped away, trying to see if there was

something wrong with his sword. His enemy followed. What was going on? With Blódbál he was supposed to be pretty much invincible against another swordsman. The sword's song rang in his head as strongly as ever.

Again the tall Indian attacked. Phoenix twisted his wrists to let the curved blade glance off Blódbál. He used the rebound momentum to add power to his overhead blow as he stepped to one side. It should have been a killing blow but it swished through empty space. The man had moved.

The extra awareness granted by Blódbál's magic gave him just enough time to turn and drop to one knee. That lethal, curved blade sang over his head from behind. Seizing the opportunity, he struck upward with his dagger. It caught on cloth. There was a tearing sound and the Indian spun aside with an angry cry. Phoenix rose and they circled each other warily.

He glanced briefly at his dagger but the blade was clean. No hit then. This guy was *fast*, and there was something familiar in the way he moved. Phoenix's eyes narrowed in sudden suspicion. He looked up again and realised he had made a fatal mistake in taking his eyes off his opponent even for a second. In that moment, his foe jumped forward. He covered the distance between them faster than Phoenix believed possible. Now only inches away, the Indian slid that curved blade between Phoenix's ribs with a deft turn of the wrist. Then he grinned.

Phoenix stared up at him and wondered why it didn't hurt yet.

As Phoenix dropped to his knees, he heard Jade's terrified cry in his head before it was masked by the sound of the Indian's voice in his ears. He leaned in and whispered.

"So you see, my master was compassionate indeed. His spells cured my leg and also counter your pathetic barbarian sword-magic." Yajat, the assassin, withdrew his sword from Phoenix's body with a contemptuous smile. "I have fulfilled my master's orders and my own honour. Now I go to kill your companions." With a swift bow and a mocking salute, he gestured to his Naga troops.

Breathless with the pain that flooded through his body, Phoenix collapsed to the ground, just one more dead amongst the thousands that littered the battlefield.

*****

High above, Jade cried out and clutched her head. Instantly, Brynn was at her side.

"What is it?" He glanced at the war below.

Jade grabbed at his hand, struggling for breath as she tried to separate her mind from those of the dying. "Phoenix has lost a life. He's gone for the moment. I'll try and contact him when he wakes up. Cadoc lost one too but he's recovered. Vasi is ok and Marcus… is alright but,…oh." She glanced up at Guatamiputra who had come to kneel by her side also.

"I'm sorry, Sopaniputra is dead, sir," she said in a choked voice.

The Raj betrayed his emotion by only the merest flicker of an eyelid and the whitening of knuckles on his sword hilt. He stood again and faced the field of battle. Around him, his generals exchanged worried looks.

"Tell Vasi, he and his men are getting left behind. The retreat must be together or the plan will not work." The Raj remained calm.

Jade nodded, even though he couldn't see her. Pushing aside her fears for Phoenix, she steadied her racing heart and closed her eyes. Phoenix's best hope was for her to help the Raj win this war. She contacted Vasi and relayed the instructions. In her minds' ear, more men died, crying out to their gods and loved ones until her head rang with their pleas for salvation and tears drowned her sight.

It was becoming harder to organise the communications. The death of the commanders and captains was something none of them had really considered. As each leader died, Jade had no way to contact his replacement. They had now lost about a fifth of their communications network and the retreating front grew ragged as commands were missed.

Seeing it, the Raj growled his next order through gritted teeth. "Tell them to break and run. We cannot wait any longer."

"My lord," one of the generals pointed at the enemy camp, "Bhumaka has only committed three quarters of his army. The war chariots are still held in reserve, as are half the elephants."

"Don't you think I can see that?" Guatamiputra snapped. "I would wait longer if I could but the day depends on a slip of a girl who looks like she's about to collapse and the untried invention of a mad foreigner. If I don't give the order now then I will sacrifice thousands of men for nothing and the day will be lost. If we have any chance of defeating Bhumaka, we must execute the next stage *now.*"

Grim, the general stood his ground. "I'm only concerned, my Raj, that we may have been betrayed. Why would Bhumaka withhold his troops unless he suspected a trap?"

The Raj stilled, eyeing his general with blank hostility. He switched his gaze to Jade for a long moment. She returned it straitly, having nothing to hide.

Guatamiputra drew a long, slow breath. "It is possible but if it is so, then so be it. We cannot change our plans at this late time. Send the order, girl." The Raj crouched before her, his face mask-like. "But if I find you or one of yours has betrayed me I will make sure you all die a slow, painful death *devi* or not. Do you understand?"

Jade grabbed at Brynn before he could leap to her defence, holding the boy at her side with Elven strength.

"It is impossible for me or my friends to betray each

other or you," she returned.

Without waiting for his response, Jade closed her eyes and sent out the command to break and run. There was a backwash of such relief from the men in her head that Jade reeled and would have fallen but for Brynn's support. The mind link broke as the spell faded.

"Here." Brynn pushed a wine skin into her hand. "Drink and eat. You have a few minutes before they engage again. Do you need your herbs?"

She shook her head. "They have to be a last resort or I'll burn everything I have before this is over."

He sent her a wide-eyed, frightened look. "Is it time for Marcus to bring up the onager yet?"

She looked down at the chaotic scene below. "I'm not sure. Run and ask him so I can relay the order to the other hills. I need to renew the spell before I can mind-speak again."

Brynn nodded and raced off.

Below, Guatamiputra's men turned and ran full-tilt toward the gentle, lower slopes of the hills. Bhumaka's men, after a moment of astonishment, chased after in exultant enthusiasm. There was a gap of fifty or more metres between the retreating forces and those following.

The battle disintegrated into scattered, running skirmishes. Screams, made thin by the distance, echoed and rolled off the slopes of the low hills. The clash of steel rang true. Horses ran loose, trailing reins and skittering away from any who tried to catch them. As the sun rose higher and the day warmed, the scent of death drifted up until even those on the top of the hills gagged on it.

Looking away from the carnage, Jade was disturbed to see the general was right. Fully a third of Bhumaka's men, most of the Naga and most of his elephants and war-chariots simply stood in formation at the northern edge of the encampment. They had not joined in the chase. They seemed to be waiting for something.

Fear clutched at Jade's heart, stealing her breath. Somehow, Bhumaka must have found out about their plan. He just waited for them to spring it so he could counter with his own. But what was his intent? Just withholding troops wouldn't prevent him from being outflanked.

Muttering the spell, she tentatively reached out. *"Phoenix?"*

There was a sense of blankness, pain and weight as Phoenix's consciousness returned.

"Jade?" His mental voice was weak. *"Oh man...that one hurt."*

"What happened?"

"Yajat." His short reply conveyed a wealth of anger. *"The man from Bhumaka's tent was Yajat. He killed me. He's so damned fast! Keep an eye out. He said he was going to come after you lot, next."*

Jade clutched at her own throat. Brynn had explained who the assassin was and how Phoenix had bested him on the night of her attack. That he should return so quickly and be able to defeat Phoenix was frightening. It meant not only was Zhudai still a power in the area, but also that Phoenix was not as invincible as he thought – even with his sword in hand.

"Where are you?" she finally asked. *"You must be behind the enemy lines now."*

"Under about five bodies, by the feel of it." He grunted mentally and she sensed he tried to shove the dead off himself. *"What's happening?"*

"The retreat is in progress. I'm waiting to hear from Marcus." She tried to stay calm. *"You have to get out of there before they start the onager."*

"No, really?" His reply was sarcastic.

"There's more." She hesitated, loath to tell him. *"I think someone betrayed us. Bhumaka has kept a third of his men, most of the Naga, elephants and chariots back. I'm pretty sure they're out of range of the onager, too. He*

knows, Phoenix. Somehow, he knows."

There was a burst of subliminal swearing and mental images too quick and gruesome to follow as Phoenix vented his feelings.

"Maybe I can sneak in, kill Bhumaka and end this thing. How long have I got?"

Before Jade could reply, Brynn came running up, panting and nodding.

"Now," he gasped. "Marcus says do it now."

CHAPTER EIGHTEEN

Jade frowned, staring down at the body-strewn sweep of land below. Somewhere out there, Phoenix was injured and half-buried. If she gave the order to fire the onager, he could die – again. If she didn't, tens of thousands of the Raj's soldiers would die instead. Gritting her teeth, she closed her eyes. Sending a fleeting apologetic thought toward Phoenix, she reached out to the remaining commanders and the onager operators and sent a simple, one-word command:

"Fire."

Loud creakings and groaning of wood and rope under stress filled the air as the sixty plus onager were wheeled to the front of the hill-command stations. Within moments, they were wound back and loaded with rocks; hot gravel and sand; clay balls filled with small metal spikes; wicker balls filled with rocks, metal spikes and burning rags. In short, they were filled with every conceivable method of killing and destroying that was available in ancient India.

Sixty great arms flung their fatal loads skyward, thumping almost in unison as they hit the crosspieces at the top of their swing. Arcing gracefully through the blue sky, sixty payloads rained fire and death onto Bhumaka's men.

Jade swallowed hard and turned her face away as the screams redoubled. She plugged her ears but it didn't help. Sick guilt weighed in her stomach, making her want to retch. Surely there must have been another way to complete their quest. Her hands shook as she accepted a drink of water from Brynn. She was weakening fast. Unless this war ended soon, she would lose another life just trying to keep Guatamiputra's communication lines open for him.

She reached out for Phoenix again, raising her head to try and see him in the melee below. Relief flowed as she felt his familiar mind-touch. *"Are you ok?"*

"Sure, as long as you consider killed, buried, blood-soaked and in peril of dying – again - while stuck behind enemy lines, 'ok'." His faint, acerbic reply reassured her.

Guatamiputra interrupted her connection, tapping her on the shoulder as he pointed out over the vast plain.

"Marcus has done well. The onagers have destroyed much of Bhumaka's army and my men have made it safely behind these hills. But why does Bhumaka still wait with the rest? I am loath to commit to the flanking manoeuvre without knowing if the man has another trick up his sleeve."

Jade followed his finger and, with her long-sighted vision, saw Bhumaka himself standing in one of the war-chariots. With arms folded across a leather and iron breastplate more decorative than functional, the Kshatrap surveyed the slaughter without emotion. Beside him in the chariot swayed the head of a large, hooded cobra. *Manasa.*

She shrank from those penetrating, lidless, bottomless dark eyes.

The Raj knelt before her. "You have met Bhumaka." It was a statement, not a question.

Jade nodded.

"Can you find out what he is thinking?" Guatamiputra let his excitement shine through as he realised the potential her ability might have.

Jade stared at him in horror. What was she supposed to do? There were too many things happening at once and she didn't have enough power left to deal with any of them effectively. Phoenix was in danger and so was she. If she touched Bhumaka, there was a chance that his pet goddess would sense her intrusion and try to control her again. The thought of being taken over by the snake-goddess made her shiver.

The Raj was right, though, if she knew what Bhumaka planned, they might be able to prevent any more losses this day. Things were rapidly coming to a head and she had to make the right decision. This war had to be done with today so they could recapture Pune and return the Sudasharna to its rightful place. Tonight was the last night of the dying moon.

The war had to end now.

Sighing, she nodded and closed her eyes. A second later, they flew open again as something Phoenix had said suddenly registered in her tired mind. Guatamiputra stared at her expectantly. Ignoring him, she grabbed Brynn and whispered in his ear, handing him the Hyllion Bagia. The boy opened his eyes wide then nodded and grinned.

Closing her eyes again, Jade reached out toward the Saka leader. His mind was a jumble of emotions: excitement; fear; worry; triumph and anticipation all warred with each other and made his intentions difficult to read. He clearly had some sort of plan in mind but Jade couldn't sort it out. Frowning, she pushed harder, seeking to find the source of his feelings of triumph when it appeared his army had been crushed.

It was tantalizingly close. She almost had it…

Darkness fell as her mind was seized by another, stronger will. A familiar cold, alien awareness wrapped itself around hers and smothered her. Then it simply took over her body. Defenceless in her weakened state, Jade felt her consciousness shunted aside as Manasa took control.

Trapped in a small corner of her own mind, she watched in terrified frustration as her body stood jerkily upright. She fought but couldn't stop her own hand as it drew her dagger. All her willpower couldn't halt her body as it stepped toward the Raj. Guatamiputra now stood with his unprotected back to her, staring down at the battlefield. Frantic, Jade pushed against the invisible walls that held her prisoner but to no avail. She tried to reach out mentally but that was blocked as well. She simply hadn't the strength to fight the goddess' control this time. She was going to kill the Raj and everyone would think she had betrayed him.

Then, faintly, the sound of a distant hunting horn rang into the blue sky: a pure, clean sound that nevertheless sent a shiver down the spine of everyone who heard it. Jade's body screamed in pain; her hands clutched at her ears. From high above, an eagle's cry sounded a shrill echo. Below, every elephant raised its trunk and trumpeted a response until the plains resounded with animal noise, all upheld by that single, unwavering note.

Seizing the moment, Jade pushed against her prison with every ounce of mental strength she had. The slick, cold bonds burst and she flooded into her own mind, pushing Manasa out again. Shaking, she sheathed her dagger and sank to the ground as her knees collapsed. She barely heard Brynn's anxious questions as he shoved the horn of Aurfanon back into the Hyllion Bagia.

Afraid Manasa would take over, Jade had instructed Brynn to blow the horn the instant she looked like doing anything odd. Obviously he considered attempting to murder the Raj sufficiently strange. Brynn tried to give back the Bag but her hands shook too much, so he shoved it into his own shirt. She nodded gratefully.

Thank goodness. It was over.

Or not…

Around her, a stir of confused babble and frightened conversation broke out. What now?

*****

Below, still half-buried, Phoenix heard the silvery note of the horn of Aurfanon and grinned to himself.

"Good girl," he muttered, shoving the last heavy body off his legs. "Now let's see what Bhumaka makes of whatever the horn summons this time."

Crouching amongst the dead, he cautiously raised his head and peered over sprawled bodies. Less than a hundred metres away, Bhumaka stood in a chariot. By his side was the swaying hood of Manasa, the giant snake-goddess. Bhumaka seemed to be yelling at her; waving his arms and pointing toward the hilltop. Obviously something had gone wrong and the Kshatrap wasn't happy.

Overhead, the sound of an eagle's melancholy shriek drifted through the sky. Phoenix glanced up, shading his eyes from the now-blinding sun. Had Jade created more eagle-illusions to deal with the goddess? It seemed unlikely. She wasn't strong enough. No, there was just one eagle circling and spiralling lower toward the battlefield. It was a big one, though. In fact... Phoenix's jaw dropped as the eagle swooped closer. It wasn't just big, it was bloody enormous – and it was coming right toward him!

Around Bhumaka, the Naga panicked, sliding off in all directions to hide from their mortal enemy. The eagle paid them no attention. Instead, it dove straight toward Phoenix, snapping its wings out at the last second and extending mighty talons. Paralysed with shock, he reacted too late. Just as he began to throw himself to one side, those claws wrapped around his torso and he was lifted off the ground with a neck-twisting jerk.

Shrieking again, the eagle laboured to gain height. Arrows now arced through the air as Bhumaka managed to rally some of his men to shoot at it. They glanced harmlessly off the glossy brown feathers. The eagle cried its defiance.

Recovering, Phoenix drew his arm back, intending to stick the point of his sword into a leg to make it let go. A sudden thought occurred to him and he glanced down with a gulp. OK. Maybe doing that at two hundred feet off the ground wasn't such a good idea after all. Maybe he should just wait and see where he was going.

It didn't take long to realise that the eagle's destination was the Raj's hill-top command centre. Relieved, Phoenix tucked his knees in and managed a decent roll as the great bird opened its talons mere inches off the ground. Coming to his feet, Phoenix caught sight of Jade's astonished stare, Brynn envious one and Guatamiputra's half-fearful one.

"Er…hi," he said, attempting to look cool and casual. He waved a hand at the dumbfounded generals. "Thanks for the rescue, Jade."

She shut her mouth with a snap and shook her head. "Brynn blew the horn."

She switched to staring at the great eagle as it landed before her and folded its wings. It stood almost twice her height with a wingspan of over forty feet. Its golden-brown feathers shone in the sunlight and it fixed an intelligent, black eye first on Jade then on the Raj. Cocking its head, it took two half-jump-steps toward Guatamiputra.

A bizarre, breathless silence fell over the entire battlefield as every soldier stopped to watch the scene playing out on the mountain above.

"Oh!" Jade's gasp of surprise broke the silence. The generals all looked at her.

"I can hear him," she tapped her temple. "He says his name is Garuda."

The Raj and all his men turned pale. Whispers began amongst all the Indians nearby and Phoenix heard the name being repeated – at first softly then more loudly as men yelled the news to their friends below. Soon, it was taken up almost as a chant of reverence. Thousands upon thousands of Indian soldiers called out the name until it swept across the plains like a swelling wave and crashed upon the opposing army's silence.

"Gar-u-da! Gar-u-da! Gar-u-da!"

Phoenix exchanged confused looks with Brynn and then with Marcus, who came over to see what was happening.

Slowly, and with great grace, the giant eagle extended one wing and one clawed foot. Next, he bent his regal head and bowed – straight toward Guatamiputra. The Raj's army below erupted into screams of delight, cheers and applause. Elephants trumpeted and horses whinnied in surprise at the noise.

On Bhumaka's side of the field, there was a vast, oppressed silence – followed by the sound of thousands of men turning to look at their leader in askance.

Vasi hurried over, his eyes wide at the sight before him. Then his face split into a huge grin and he clapped Phoenix on the shoulder.

"Don't you see?" he yelled when Phoenix raised an uncomprehending eyebrow at him. "This is Garuda – the eagle upon which the god Vishnu himself rides. Legends say that Garuda will only recognise a *true* king. Both armies can see he has bowed only to my father, not to the western Kshatrap. Naga Goddess on his side or not, Bhumaka cannot dispute with Vishnu and Garuda. My father is Raj, not him. We have won."

Phoenix grabbed his arm and pointed toward the battlefield. "Not yet we haven't. Your men may believe but it doesn't look like Bhumaka, Manasa and their people are ready to give up just yet. We still have a war on our hands."

Sure enough, Bhumaka was exhorting his commanders to fight. Slowly, the orders filtered down through the ranks and the front row of soldiers turned back to the battle at hand – but there was an unmistakable reluctance in their moves now; a slowness to swing or engage that hadn't been there previously.

Phoenix turned to Guatamiputra. "I think now would be a good time to bring out the flanking reinforcements.

Most of Bhumaka's men are just farmers and slaves. Marcus' onager have terrified them and Garuda has broken what little belief they had in their leader. Now is the time to reinforce that. Maybe they'll quit."

The Raj nodded and gave Jade the order. Looking pale, she closed her eyes and passed it on. From behind the three hills, a hundred and twenty thousand men, a thousand armoured elephants and twenty thousand war chariots emerged; shaking the ground like an earthquake.

Garuda now turned back to Jade and tilted his head the other way.

She sighed and nodded. "I know."

Phoenix glanced back and forth between them. "What do you know?"

She shrugged one shoulder. "Remember the painting on the wall of the temple Vasi told you about? Well, here's the big eagle and," she nodded to Brynn. He reached into his shirt, into the Bag and handed over the shining silver disc given to them by Anuket, "here's the Sudarshana. I guess it's time to go flying."

Vasi gasped at the sight of the long-lost totem. "You had it all along and you didn't say anything? Why?"

Phoenix restrained him as he tried to step forward and take it from Jade. "Our Quest all along has been to return it to the statue in Punya-Vishnaya. Then, when you told us about the painting, we kinda figured there might be a few other things we had to do along the way. Telling you and the Raj would have complicated things. Would you have let us keep it or would you have taken it and tried to use it as a weapon, yourselves?"

Vasi looked abashed but didn't move when Phoenix released him. They watched as Jade clambered awkwardly onto the great eagle's neck and clutched at the glossy feathers.

Phoenix felt a nudge and looked down. Brynn had elbowed him.

"She's really not very well, you know," he said pointedly.

Phoenix glanced up as Garuda skipped to the edge of the mountain plateau and unfolded his wings. Jade was paler than usual, that was certain.   But who wouldn't be nervous at the prospect of flying without a seatbelt – or even a seat.

"She'll be fine once this is over and we return the Sudarshana," he assured the boy.

"Where's Cadoc?" Brynn demanded, looking around.

Garuda took off and the watchers gasped at the sweep of his massive, majestic wings. Little swirls of dust arose from the ground beneath.

Phoenix shrugged, awed by the sight, shading his eyes against the sun to follow Garuda's path.

"Somewhere down on the plain, still, I guess. I lost sight of him early on. He was fighting with Sopaniputra."

"Sopaniputra's dead," Brynn reported casually, watching Jade. "Hey, doesn't that make Vasi the heir to the throne now?"

Grimacing, Phoenix turned to see if Vasi had heard. He had. His face was ashen and set with a curiously reluctant, almost unhappy look. Without a word, he spun on his heel and stalked over to his father.

"Good one, kid." Phoenix cuffed Brynn on the head.

CHAPTER NINETEEN

Jade gulped and closed her eyes. Tucking the Sudarshana into her shirt, she unconsciously tightened her grip on Garuda's smooth feathers with each flap of those giant wings. She'd never been a good traveller and the eagle's jerky flight made her stomach roil and her mouth fill with saliva. She swallowed, deciding that he probably wouldn't appreciate her chucking on his nice, clean feathers.

They gained altitude and she shivered in the thin, cold air. Garuda banked in a tight circle. Jade gulped and peeked with one eye. The ground was a long, long way down. She gasped and clutched a handful of feather, crushing them until he sent her a gentle, mental protest.

"Sorry," she called. Her words were swept away in the wind. She muttered the mind-talk spell and switched to telepathy. *"Sorry. What do I do now?"*

"I will fly low over Bhumaka's men and you will hold up the Sudarshana for them to see." Came the reply. Garuda's mind-voice sounded old, many-layered and amused – as though the doings of men were affording him some sort of obscure hilarity only he understood.

"That's it?" It couldn't be so simple.

"That's it. Vishnu and I will take care of the rest," the great bird replied.

Then he began his descent and Jade was too preoccupied in trying to hang on without breaking any feathers to protest further. Garuda tucked his wings in slightly and arrowed toward the ground, gathering speed. Without realising it, she opened her mouth, yelling in terror as the ground rushed toward them.

"Hold on." His instruction was tinged with laughter.

"What else would I be doing?" she replied tartly, shutting her mouth with a snap.

Less than two hundred metres above the battlefield, Garuda stretched out his great wings again. Jade's head rocked on her shoulders. Wind ruffled and fluttered his pinions like golden flags.

Fumbling a little, she pulled out the Sudarshana and held it high in both hands. Hopefully, something amazing would happen, otherwise she was just going to look extremely silly.

"Turn the engraved side to face Bhumaka's army," Garuda instructed.

She obliged, directing the correct flat, circular side toward the mystified Saka army.

"Nothing's happening!" she cried.

"Patience," was the amused reply.

"But what if-" Her question was obliterated as a great blast of non-sound and purple-blue-white light exploded from the Sudarshana.

Like a rolling wall, it pushed through the air toward Bhumaka's men. Men and animals flew backward. Chariots upturned. Elephants fell over, their thick legs scrabbling in the air. Ten-stakes and fence-posts were uprooted as the wave hit and passed through the Saka army like a tornado. In its wake, men and animals were left groaning but intact. Every weapon, however, every sword, shield, arrow, spike and piece of armour crumbled to dust as soon as their owners stood up. Bhumaka's men were left completely defenceless, bewildered and frightened.

Their wails rose in one vast miasma of fear.

After a brief moment of astonishment, Guatamiputra's

army let out a massive cheer. The front line ran forward, ready to fall on their unarmed enemy.

"Stop them," Garuda commanded Jade.

Glad to prevent more bloodshed, she focussed on the commanders and captains. *"Hold!"*

The Raj's army faltered to a halt, glancing uncertainly at each other as the order went around.

"Good, now to bring them clarity of vision," Garuda ordered, his tone regretful.

He raised his head and let out a long, wailing shriek. In her hands, the chakra vibrated as it picked up the sound and magnified it. Once more, a great wall of power erupted from the weapon and swept across the stunned men below.

Jade almost dropped the Sudarshana as the backlash of sorrow hit her. Tears rolled down her cheeks unbidden. All around was carnage; wasted life; stupidity; greed; desire for wealth and power at the cost of thousands of vibrant, human beings.

Why? All for one man's personal gain; personal power; personal wealth.

Bhumaka did this not for his people but for his own sake – so he could strip the people and the land of its riches and wallow in the luxury they provided. He placed his own health and happiness over theirs. Even his agreement with the Naga would only benefit him, since he never intended to honour his side of their bargain. When the war was over, if Bhumaka was victorious, the only winner would be himself.

Even then, it would still not be enough. Nothing could truly fill the void in his soul: the aching, deep lack of self-esteem that led him to destroy lives in an effort to fulfil his own. He would never be happy inside but he would spend years and thousands of lives in a futile effort to find it outside himself.

All of this knowledge flashed into her mind in a few, brief seconds but it was enough for Jade to understand

Bhumaka's deepest fears and driving forces. There was no doubt, either, that this same understanding had been conveyed instantly to every single man in his army.

Almost in unison, an army of men turned to look at their leader in appalled silence. Bhumaka, standing on a hastily-righted chariot, cringed away from their stares. Beside him, Manasa hissed and flicked her forked tongue at him. There were a few, long moments of profound silence. Then, one by one, the men of Bhumaka's army turned their backs and began to walk away. Slowly, in pairs and small groups, they ignored the few commanding officers who gave orders and collected their things for the long march back over the mountain range – back to their farms and families.

For awhile, Jade could only watch in astonishment as an entire army silently dissolved before her eyes. Where, minutes before, there had been outright war, now there was nothing but silent determination to be done and gone. She looked toward the top of the hill, wondering what Guatamiputra thought of everything. He was too far away to make out clearly.

"It is almost time for you to return the Sudarshana to its rightful place, child," Garuda said, sounding weary.

Jade twisted around toward the western horizon. Sure enough, the sun hung low in the sky, shimmering redly through the afternoon haze. Just beneath it, barely visible against its glare, the sliver-crescent of the waning moon kissed the mountains.

"I'll never get to Punya-Vishnaya before the moon disappears!"

"There is enough time. I will drop you near the Pataleshwar cave temple," Garuda assured her. *"Tell your friends to ride and meet you there. They should make it in time, too. Just make sure you find the idol of Vishnu in the temple of Shiva before the moon vanishes."*

He flapped his great wings and headed toward the

river. Jade sent the message and soon spotted Phoenix, Marcus and Brynn galloping madly across the plain toward the town. She glanced back over her shoulder. Bhumaka's army still flowed away toward the west but Manasa and her Naga had not joined them. Instead, they stared after Garuda as he flew away. Jade really wasn't very keen on having them behind her friends. They might be disaffected with Bhumaka but they probably still carried a grudge against the treasure-hunters who'd attacked them.

"What about the Naga and Manasa," she asked.

There was an impression of both amusement and resignation in Garuda's reply. *"You do your job and let me do mine. I have a score to settle with Manasa diva. She and I are old adversaries. Our battle has raged for thousands of years and will do so into the future but she and hers will not trouble you again."*

Jade didn't know quite what to make of that, so she sat dumb as Garuda's wingstrokes covered the last few hundred metres. He settled in the dirt courtyard of a temple complex in the middle of the small farming community. It was a tight fit and his backwinging sent up huge whorls of dust into the air, making her cough and sputter. Eyes watering, she slid down to the ground and backed away.

"Um… thank you," she said, looking at his expressionless, regal face.

He bowed his head. *"And I thank you, child. Return the Sudarshana and balance to this land, if you will. I will be glad to have some rest."* With that cryptic utterance, the eagle crouched low and launched himself skyward again with a final cry.

Shading her eyes, Jade watched him go and sighed. Riding on the back of a giant eagle - now *that* was something you didn't do often in any world.

"Right," she said briskly, glancing around the deserted courtyard. "So where's this statue of Vishnu then?"

"Right in there," came a deep, familiar voice nearby.

"Cadoc!" Jade cried, running toward him. "You're here. Where are the others?" She looked around him, searching for the rest of her companions.

The Player shrugged. "I got here first. They'll be here shortly."

Taking her hand, he smiled down at her but there was a strained look about his eyes. He looked tired. His clothes were darkened with blood and slashed in several places. The war had not been kind to him.

She caught a glimpse of his ruby-studded arm band. There was only one red stone left.

"Oh, Cadoc!" she said impulsively. "I forgot. You're on your last life. I'm so sorry."

He shrugged. "No matter. I'm sure I'll get some back somehow, soon. But c'mon. We need to get that Sudarshana in place before the moon vanishes. The statue of Vishnu's in here." He waved a hand toward a large, ornately-carved square stone building in the centre of the temple compound.

Pulling back against his grip, she dug her heels in and twisted free. "Hang on. I'd rather wait a few minutes until the others get here. Phoenix should be part of this. It's our quest."

Cadoc sent her a swift, frowning look. "But if you wait you might miss the moon and lose the chance to finish it at all. Don't be silly." He reached out for her again but Jade backed away.

There was something wrong. He wasn't acting right. She narrowed her eyes and tilted her head to one side, staring at him hard with more than just her eyes.

"What's going on, Cadoc?" Uneasy, she took another step away.

He grinned but it was a forced imitation of his usual bright smile. "Nothing at all. I've finished my quest and I'm just helping you to finish yours. Is that a crime?"

Jade stared at him for a moment, trying to work out

what caused her to feel so ill at ease with him. Then it clicked.

"How did you know about our quest?" She backed further away. "We never told you because we didn't want to get deleted. How did you know about the Sudarshana and the moon?"

Cadoc hesitated then laughed. "Phoenix told me, of course. When you were sleeping. And I told him what my quest was. We decided it was worth the risk."

"So what was yours then?" she shot back.

He shrugged. "It doesn't matter now. It's done. Now let's finish yours and get to the next level. C'mon. The statue is just through that door."

Jade looked at the dark, rectangular opening set between ornate columns carved into a stone wall. A feeling of foreboding came over her and she shook her head.

"I'll wait for the others, thanks."

Cadoc took a half-step toward her, visibly controlled himself and stopped with a one-shoulder shrug. "Whatever. But the moon's just about gone, so I wouldn't wait too long."

She risked a quick look over her shoulder. Sure enough, as the sun's light reddened across the plains, the last faint glimmer of the thin crescent moon hung in the sky above the mountain peaks in the west. He was right. She couldn't afford to wait any longer.

Cadoc leaned against a column with apparent unconcern, picking his nails with one of his throwing knives. Maybe she was just being over-cautious, as usual. She was tired and reading too much into his desire to be done with this level and get on to the next. After all, he'd looked after her so thoughtfully over the last few days when she was feeling ill... Jade hesitated, biting her lip.

She glanced at the moon again. It was now almost completely invisible in the dusky sky. She really didn't have time to wait. Slipping her dagger discretely out of its sheath, she nodded to Cadoc and followed him into the temple.

As she stepped through the door, Jade extended her senses, listening hard for any unexpected, hidden enemies. She only got the impression of a large, empty room. There was no-one waiting inside except Cadoc. It must have been the stress of the day playing on her mind; making her paranoid about a friend's intentions. She spelled a dozen green dancing lights into existence and sent them floating around. Even that small magic left her weakened.

In the centre of the square room was a large statue of a man sitting cross-legged. In one hand he held a three-pronged trident while the other was upraised, palm-outward. Around his neck hung a cobra and a long, bead necklace. A moon-shape device decorated his long hair; there was a third eye in the middle of his forehead and he seemed to be sitting on a tiger-skin.

Jade looked askance at Cadoc, who shook his head.

"That's Shiva. I looked him up. He's The Destroyer or the Transformer," Cadoc grimaced. "Bit hard to tell if the Indians think he's a good god or a bad one. He seems to have both aspects. Hinduism is amazingly complicated." He flashed Jade a grin. "I was trying to explain it to my little brother and he decided that must be why the Indians are so keen on cricket – because it's easier to understand."

Jade laughed aloud then covered her mouth as the sound echoed weirdly in the huge, cubic space. "So who are the others? Where's Vishnu?" she whispered.

Cadoc pointed in turn to the shadowed statue of an elephant-headed man; an archer with a woman beside him; a beautiful, four-armed woman carrying lotus flowers; and finally a large, four-armed man carrying a mace, a lotus flower and a shell.

"That's Ganesh, Remover of Obstacles; then there's the hero Rama and his wife, Sita; next is Lakshmi, goddess of wealth and also Vishnu's wife and that's Vishnu himself with the shell and flower. See, his fourth hand is empty?" Cadoc gave her a little shove in the back. "Go on, return the Chakra and finish your quest."

Jade stepped forward, still reluctant to do this without the others. She paused, listening for the sound of hoofbeats in the hopes that they would turn up at the last second. There was only silence and the sound of her own and Cadoc's breathing.

Abruptly, a shaft of red sunlight pierced the green-black gloom of the temple. Looking up, she saw a crescent-shaped hole cut in the wall. The sliver of the dying moon fit precisely into it. The reddish beam fell onto Vishnu's motionless form. She sighed. If she'd been waiting for a sign to say exactly when it was time to fulfil her part of the quest, it didn't get much clearer than that. Pulling out the Sudarshana, she crossed the last few steps to the statue and gently slipped the chakra into Vishnu's open hand. It fitted; shining silver in the light.

Nothing happened.

Jade frowned. Maybe nothing dramatic was supposed to happen but somehow she didn't think so. She couldn't imagine the game programmers writing a dull ending for a successful quest. Looking closely at the chakra, she rolled her eyes at her own stupidity and turned it around so the engraved side faced outward. Now there would be fireworks, for sure.

Stepping back, she collided with Cadoc. He had come silently up behind her. She jumped away with an apology but he wasn't paying attention. His gaze was fixed on the statue. Jade watched as well, bewildered by his strange attitude. What was he looking for?

CHAPTER TWENTY

Phoenix, Marcus and Brynn galloped into the Pune temple complex with the sun casting their shadows long behind them. Had Jade made it? Were they too late to put the Sudarsharna back in its place? They'd ridden as fast as they could to get here. What happened if they'd failed this Quest? Would they be stuck here on Level four forever?

As his stallion clattered to a stop before the dark, gaping entrance to the temple, Phoenix held his breath. He swung down from the saddle and peered around into the darkness.

A white figure came sprinting out of the temple: Jade, her hair flying and a delighted grin on her face. She flung her arms around him and gave him an enthusiastic hug.

"You made it!" she carolled, turning to the others as their mounts came to a stop as well.

Brynn was almost thrown forward over his mare's neck. He slid to the ground with a groan, clutching his backside. "I think I'll walk from now on, if you don't mind."

Jade laughed and gave him a quick hug, then sent Marcus a warm look.

Phoenix threw his reins over a low post nearby.

"Sorry we're late. We got held up by some looters in the village. Vasi and the Raj sent their thanks and farewells, by the way. Oh, and you left this behind." He tossed Jade's staff to her.

She caught it with a grin. Marcus strode over and grabbed her arms as though worried she would run away. He looked sharply at her face, pale in the moonlight.

"Are you well?"

Jade smiled. "Fine. A little tired. I didn't wait for you, though. I had to return the Sudarshana at the right time. It's done."

Phoenix blinked at her. "What? It's all over, just like that? No fireworks, no explosions, no badguy? Where is the statue?"

Jade shrugged. "I know. It's all a bit of an anticlimax after the battle. It's inside. Cadoc's there, too."

"Cadoc!" Brynn pushed past her. "You left him in there with the statue and the Sudarshana?"

"Sure," she replied sending him a quizzical look. "He's the one who led me to it in time. Why?"

Without further word, Brynn darted inside the darkened temple, leaving the others to exchange shrugs.

The sun set with a final, firey flash, softening the evening into purple gloom.

"He doesn't trust Cadoc," Phoenix explained.

"What?" Jade gaped at him. "He's practically waited on me hand and foot for the last three days. He's lost a life in a war he didn't need to be involved in. He helped us complete our quest. What else does Brynn want?"

But Phoenix caught a flash of doubt in her expression; a hint of uncertainty in her protestations. Why? Had Cadoc done something to make her doubt his integrity?

At that second, Brynn's high-pitched voice carried to them out of the darkness.

"Put it *back* you thief! Put it back before you ruin every-" There was an ominous thump and Brynn's words were cut off in mid-sentence.

Phoenix drew Blódbál and dove into the dark opening. He rolled and came up on one knee, looking for trouble. Not far away, he found it. Brynn was a limp, silent shape lying in a corner of the room. Bathed in the last, lingering hints of sunlight, Cadoc stood in front of a large, four-armed statue. He held the Sudarshana and smiled with satisfaction. Tucking it into his haversack, he reached for the conch shell.

"Hey!" Phoenix yelled. "What do you think you're doing?"

Cadoc sent a scornful look over his shoulder. "What does it look like? I'm taking what I need to win the next level."

"But…but…" Phoenix stuttered.

Jade and Marcus appeared behind him and he sensed their astonishment.

"But what," Cadoc scoffed. "Did you really think I was helping you just so I could lose another life and be a do-gooder. Please." He jerked his head at the statue. "These four weapons will get me through the last level even on one life."

"But…" Phoenix trailed off, not knowing what to say. "We would have helped you through the next level if you'd asked."

"Oh, don't be more of a fool than you have to be." Cadoc's mouth twisted with disdain. "My next level is in Rome. How would you have helped me? You're going to China."

Phoenix shut his teeth with a snap. "How did you know that?"

The other Player laughed. "I know everything about your quest."

"How?" Phoenix growled, stepping into the room.

Cadoc slipped a throwing knife into his hand and hefted it. "Don't come any closer. I can take your last few lives without blinking."

Phoenix froze, knowing only too well how accurate he was with those knives.

"And don't try any magic, either, Jade," Cadoc

warned, flicking a glance her way. "You're so weak you won't be able to do more than those little witchlights of yours, anyway."

"Huh?" Jade's blank confusion echoed Phoenix's.

"You lot really are gullible, you know that?" The Breton prince continued eyeing them both with a scornful expression.

Phoenix heard Jade gasp.

"It wasn't Leela's spices. It was you," she whispered. "You drugged us that night on the mountain. Oh! All those cups of tea and wine you kept giving me. The weakness I've been feeling. You were poisoning me, you pig! I've lost *three* lives because of you. You're working for Bhumaka! *That's* how we got away from him so easily. *That's* how he knew about the battle plan, too. You… you…" She sputtered to a halt, obviously overcome by anger.

"Very good," Cadoc said condescendingly. "You are the smartest one in the bunch – just not smart enough. You're almost right."

"We trusted you," Marcus put in, his voice low and harsh.

"More fool you," the Player retorted. "This is a game and I aim to win. You lot waste too much time worrying about doing the right thing when you should just be doing whatever it takes to win."

"So what do you get out of all this?" Marcus asked.

Cadoc laughed. "You mean besides four of the most powerful weapons in this world? Money, of course, and more lives."

"How?" "Who from?" Phoenix and Marcus spoke together.

"Bhumaka and my master." A new voice spoke from the darkness beside Cadoc. Into the faint, greenish light of Jade's spells stepped Yajat. His dark eyes glittered strangely in the half-light. He laid a hand on Cadoc's shoulder and squeezed until the younger man flinched. "Cadoc has served both Bhumaka and the Dragonmaster. Although I suspect Bhumaka may not be in a position to fulfil *his* half of the deal, Cadoc will be suitably rewarded by *my* master." Yajat's deep voice held a hint of irony.

Phoenix heard Jade draw a sharp breath and wondered what she realised that he didn't. Whatever it was, it would have to wait. The priority had to be getting that chakra back in place. They didn't have much time before their quest was over in all the wrong ways.

"Wait!" Phoenix commanded as Cadoc turned again and reached for the conch shell in Vishnu's hand. "At least leave the chakra long enough for our quest to be completed."

Yajat smiled and Cadoc laughed again. "Phoenix, I've been paid large sums to *prevent* your quest from succeeding; to kill Jade; to kill Sopaniputra and to help Bhumaka win this war. You've managed to stop me from completing two of my tasks. There is no way I'm going to leave the Sudarshana in place and let you get to Level Five. Zhudai would kill me."

Jade took a half-step toward him. "But-"

Before she could complete the sentence, Yajat's hand moved and the handle of a long knife suddenly sprouted from Cadoc's stomach. The assassin looked coolly on as Cadoc stared first at him then at his own body in bewildered shock. The Player coughed and a small dribble of blood appeared on his lip.

"Wha...?" He sank to his knees and blinked up at Yajat. "You bast-"

The assassin withdrew the knife and wiped it clean on Cadoc's shirt before returning it to the sheath at his belt.

"You didn't seriously expect the Dragonmaster to reward you so richly when you admit you failed at half of your tasks?" Yajat pressed his two hands together in front of his face and bowed. "Namaste. May you return as something more worthy in your next life: perhaps a cockroach."

Cadoc coughed again; the breath rattling in his throat. His eyes closed as his body slumped. He fell to earth with a thump and his corpse vanished in deep shadows beneath the statue.

Jade's disbelieving voice broke the silence. "That…that was his last life. He's…gone."

Shaken, Phoenix renewed his grip on his sword. Blodbal sang its war-song, urging him to action, to death, to glory. He shook his head, trying to push thoughts of death - his or Cadoc's aside. At least Cadoc, traitor though he was, still had a real life on the outside. Unless they were very careful, Yajat could do the same thing to Jade or Phoenix himself - and there was no telling what would happen when they lost their last lives.

"Phoenix," Marcus drew his weapon, "we need to get the Sudarshana back into the statue's hand – now."

Phoenix shook himself, tearing his gaze away from Cadoc's motionless body.

Jade raised her staff, glaring at Yajat. "Right. Let's do it. Three to one, even if I can't do magic, is pretty good odds."

Yajat threw back his head and laughed aloud. The sound echoed oddly in the stone room. "You don't really think I came alone, do you?"

At a gesture, six, black-clad men emerged from the shadows. Green witchlight glinted off an assortment of evil-looking hooked, clawed and bladed weapons.

"Not good," Phoenix muttered.

Seven trained assassins against three. Not good odds at all. He flexed his neck, feeling various bruises and injuries from the day's fighting and riding.

The assassins closed in, moving on silent feet. There was a chill feeling of anticipation and breathless fear in the room. Jade's witchlights flickered and dimmed.

"Jade?" Phoenix said, trying to see her and the assassins at the same time.

"I'm sorry." Her voice sounded fainter. "Cadoc was right. I tried but I've got nothing left. I can still fight, though." She stepped in to fill the space beside Marcus.

"Stay together," Phoenix instructed. The others nodded and the three companions turned outward to face their adversaries as one.

Still unnervingly silent, the black-clad fighters sprang forward. Phoenix let the song of the sword flood through his mind, allowing it to control his muscles. He moved faster than he believed he ever could to block the first two strikes. The sharp *ktchang* of metal hurt his eardrums as it echoed off stone. His heart raced. He twisted sideways to avoid one strike. He stepped back again before they could open a gap between him and the others. A knife flew past his head, barely missing his ear. Too close.

In that moment of distraction, he almost didn't see the *katar* punch-blade aimed at his stomach. Sucking in his gut, he managed to deflect the arm that held it. He jabbed at the wielder's jaw with the hilt of Blódbál. There was a *crunch* as solid metal connected with flesh and bone. The assassin staggered back, clutching at his face. Yajat growled at him. The man shook his head and re-entered the fray.

A loud, hollow *crack* attested to Jade's skill with the quarterstaff and one opponent went down at her feet, unconscious. Behind Phoenix, Marcus breathed raggedly as he fended off two antagonists at once. One man pitched forward and almost fell on top of Phoenix. He gave the man a thump across the head with the hilt of his sword for good measure and shoved the body aside, wondering what had happened. He'd been nowhere near any of their weapons. A flicker of movement behind Vishnu's statue told him Brynn must have woken and was doing his best with his sling.

There was no more time to wonder about his companions. Two antagonists came at Phoenix together, one swinging high, the other low. It was impossible to block both. No could he dodge without opening up the tight defensive position he and the others kept. He made a split-second decision and sidestepped slightly forward to the left to avoid the low strike and pre-empt the high one. Sliding his left hand up the chest of that assassin, he caught the man under the chin with the palm of his hand. With Blódbál, Phoenix blocked a new sword-strike from the first assailant, even as he dropped to one knee and drove the second killer into the stone floor with his left hand. The man didn't get up. One down.

Snatching his dagger out, Phoenix relaxed his sword-arm. Losing balance, the assassin leaned just a little too far forward. Driving from his toes, Phoenix used his upward momentum to slide under his opponent's upraised guard. He jammed the dagger to the hilt into an exposed ribcage. The man staggered back, gasping.

Glancing around, he saw Marcus had successfully dealt with his second attacker and was busy helping Jade. In moments, only the three companions were left standing. Around them lay the limp bodies of half a dozen of Yajat's men. Grinning, Phoenix straightened up to look at this last foe. Maybe there was a chance they could do this, after all.

Yajat leaned casually against Vishnu's leg. He began clapping slowly.

"Well done, well done." He hitched himself off the stone figure and sauntered toward them. Tilting his head, he eyed Phoenix with respect. "I was disappointed when I killed you so easily on the battlefield but perhaps you really are everything I was told."

"What are you talking about?" Phoenix said impatiently. "We don't have time to waste chatting. Your men are beaten and so are you. If you leave now we won't have to kill you. Go back to Zhudai and tell him we're coming."

Yajat waggled a finger at him. "Surely you are not going to make the same mistake twice, my friend? You cannot let me go. You will have to fight for your freedom, and I will be honoured to take the last lives of a skilled martial artist."

"Look," Phoenix sighed, "we've just defeated your men and you know I can beat you, so let's just call it quits. I've had a long day."

"But you are mistaken," Yajat said quietly.

"About what? Beating your men or beating you?" Phoenix waved a scornful hand at the prostrate bodies on the floor. "Because I *know* it's been a long day."

"Both." The assassin smiled. He raised his hand.

Out from the shadows stepped thirty more silent, deadly warriors. One of them had his elbow firmly locked around Brynn's throat. The boy's feet barely touched the ground. His fingernails scrabbled at the arm across his windpipe.

"Put down your weapons, or the boy dies now." Yajat's voice was no longer light and friendly. He was now deadly serious.

Phoenix exchanged a questioning look with Jade and Marcus, both of whom nodded. Together they slowly laid their weapons on the floor and raised their hands above their heads.

Yajat smiled contemptuously. "Cadoc was right. You are gullible do-gooders. I cannot believe you have managed to stay alive this long." He walked past the man holding Brynn and nodded.

"Kill him."

The knife plunged toward the boy's throat.

CHAPTER TWENTY-ONE

In mid-stroke, the assassin's arm faltered. The blade fell from his hand and clattered to the floor. With a peculiar, shocked expression on his face, he released Brynn and slid bonelessly to the ground. A knife handle protruded from his back.

Quicker than thought, Brynn took advantage of the moment of confusion and darted across to the dubious shelter of his companions. From beneath Jade's arm, he joined them in staring at the dead man.

"Who did that?" Yajat turned on his men in fury. "Who?"

"I did," came a familiar voice from the shadows.

Cadoc stepped into the light. He sauntered over to stand next to Jade and Brynn. Phoenix glared at him, wondering what he was up to now.

Yajat started. "You were out of lives. You told me so. I saw your life-bracelet. How have you returned?"

Cadoc shrugged. "I lied. I do that, sometimes. In fact, fairly often, now that I think about it. Mostly to you. I had a pretty blue potion that restored a life. Figured you might not be a completely honest and trustworthy business partner, so I lied. So kill me. Oh, wait," he cocked his head at Yajat, "you already did that."

Yajat looked at him for a long moment and shrugged. "It doesn't matter. Three or five against thirty. You are outnumbered." He turned to his men with a nod. "Kill them."

"What? Hang on a minute!" Phoenix yelped.

Yajat held up a hand. His men paused. Phoenix spoke, buying time but for what, he didn't know.

"Aren't you going to rant and rave and explain your evil plan to us? Isn't that what badguys *do?* Don't you have to stick to the script?"

Yajat raised an eyebrow at them. "What are you talking about? There is no script. My master wants you dead. Why would I waste time debating his plans with dead people? Kill them but leave that one," he pointed at Phoenix, "for me." He stepped forward.

His men paced alongside then launched themselves at the five companions.

Phoenix swore softly. Yajat laughed aloud, swinging his long, curved sword in a lethal arc toward Phoenix's head. Hampered by the need to stay close to his friends, Phoenix could do little more than block and shove the assassin back with his superior strength. Blódbál's song swelled, the fire in his blood built as his anger at the Indian grew. He gritted his teeth, trying to focus on the fight, not let the sword overwhelm his thinking.

Yajat disengaged and swung again. Phoenix had no time to wonder how the others were doing. Their only hope was if he could take Yajat out. Maybe if the head of the snake was removed, the minions would run away. Until then, he just had to hope his friends could hold out against thirty trained assassins. He didn't dare take his eyes off Yajat, even for a second, to check.

He slipped aside from Yajat's stroke, feinting a jab with his own sword, hoping to draw the assassin close enough for a dagger-strike to the gut. Instead, an underling leapt into the gap, wielding a wickedly hooked blade. He raised it to slash down at Phoenix but stopped as a metal point pierced through his chest from behind. Soundlessly, the underling slid to the ground in a heap. Yajat shoved the body aside.

"I told you, he's mine."

Phoenix rolled his eyes. "Just can't get good help these days, I guess," he taunted.

Yajat shrugged. "There's more where he came from. Where were we?"

"I think you were about to attempt to kill me and I was about to succeed at killing you." Phoenix shifted his weight, eyeing the assassin's body language closely. What attack would he use?

White teeth showed in Yajat's dark face. He danced lightly forward, his left hand hidden behind him as his right swept the flashing sword around in fancy, impressive circles. Phoenix paused, half-remembering discussions between his sensei and the senior belts - something about the hidden hand. What was it? Oh yes, watch for the knife held backward in the hidden hand. That's what Yajat was doing, trying to distract him from the knife hand. Smiling grimly, Phoenix let his focus widen, taking in the assassin's whole body, trying not to let the sword movement keep his attention too thoroughly. He dropped his own left hand back and quickly reversed his own dagger-grip. Now the blade protruded backward.

When Yajat pounced forward and struck an obvious side-blow toward Phoenix's neck, instead of waiting for it or raising his sword to block it - a move that would have exposed his right side to the hidden dagger - Phoenix moved first. He stepped in closer, intercepting the swinging arm at shoulder height with his own dagger-hand. Slicing up, he used the dagger to block. It both stopped the strike and cut through the tendonds of the assassin's sword arm. At the same time he extended his right arm and laid the edge of Blodbal's blade along Yajat's exposed throat.

Yajat's sword clattered to the ground. Jerking his head away with a growl, he swung his left hand up, dagger blade glittering in the half-light. Phoenix turned away, out of reach, wrapped his left arm around Yajat's now-useless right one and twisted it up into an arm-bar. He held Blódbál's point at the assassin's throat and forced the arm up, straightening it painfully. Yajat yelped, glaring and panting, his dagger hand flailing.

"Drop the knife and tell your friends to back off," Phoenix ordered.

Yajat sneered. "Look around and tell me who should be giving the orders."

Phoenix turned them both together. His heart sank. Every one of his friends, and Cadoc were all held firmly by at least two or three black-clad assassins. A knife at every throat. Every life in his hands. A standoff but he had more to lose. Dammit.

Suddenly, Cadoc laughed aloud. The sound cut jarringly through the silent tension of the room. Phoenix cast him an irritated glance.

"*You* may think you're in charge, Yajat but there's someone else here who may want to argue that." The Player pointed over Yajat's shoulder.

Phoenix followed his finger and his mouth fell open in surprise. Looming behind Yajat was a very large, blue-skinned, four-armed man. In one hand he held a shell, in one a lotus flower and in one, a very large, very heavy-looking mace. He glowed faintly, illuminated the room. The plinth behind him was empty.

An awed murmur swept through Yajat's men. As one, they fell to their knees, dropping weapons in an ear-shattering clatter. Phoenix released Yajat and the assassin staggered back two steps clutching his wounded arm then recovered and bowed.

"Vishnu, you honour us with your presence, lord."

"Yajat." The god gave the assassin's name a wealth of meaning – none of it good. Yajat bowed deeper until his head almost touched his knees.

"Take your men and leave. These people are under my

protection now." Vishnu's voice held the depth of caverns and the emptiness of outer space. His measured, weary tones were layered with an understanding of men and the universe that clearly weighed on his soul. There was no arguing with him.

The assassin cast the companions a venomous glance. Reluctantly, he waved at his followers. Trembling and bowing, they preceded their fuming master out the door, leaving the companions to face another god.

"Come." The god waved them forward with his empty hand. "You are safe now."

Together, the group edged forward, not quite sure of his definition of "safe" or of their reception with this enigmatic being. Thor had been bluff and good-natured – once he'd stopped trying to kill them with lightning. Anuket had been gentle and kind. Somehow they sensed that Vishnu was a far greater, more powerful being than either of those two – and probably far less tolerant.

Vishnu stretched out his empty hand toward Cadoc. "I believe you have something of mine?"

"Ah! Yes." Cadoc pulled the Sudarshana out of his backpack and handed it over with a shrug. "Sorry about that. Had to try, you know."

Vishnu hefted the great silver disc and looked straitly at him. "Perhaps I should use this on you? A little soul-searching might make you less likely to betray friends in the future."

The Player backed away, raising his hands defensively. "No thanks. I've learned my lesson – really."

The god raised one brow at him but said no more. He bowed his head toward the others, his ornately-jewelled headdress sparkling in the dim light.

"You have succeeded in returning the chakra to me. Now it is time for your next journey to begin."

"What?" Brynn's resentful question took everyone by surprise. "We go through all that...fighting and bloodshed to get that bloody thing back to you and you don't even say 'thanks'? Well, that's nice that is."

Vishnu turned his head, his bottomless eyes fixed unblinkingly on Brynn. The boy flinched.

"What thanks would you have, child? Is your life not enough?" There was no humour in the question. The god was all seriousness.

Jade pushed Brynn behind her. "Of course it's enough, sir. He's just tired. We've had a long day." Obviously hearing Brynn's indignant intake of breath, she changed the subject. "What's our next task, sir?"

Vishnu looked at her from beneath half-lowered eyelids. "You know what it is. You must master the Yu Dragon and defeat the Dragonmaster, himself – Zhudai."

"But…" Jade spread her hands. "Aren't you going to give us some weapon or tool? Some other task to complete that will help us? We're not ready to face him. We're…we're tired and we've lost too many lives. Zhudai has ways to counter Phoenix's sword. My magic is almost useless. If we go to China now, we can't possibly win…It's not fair…we can't…" Her voice trailed off and her expression tightened.

Phoenix saw her struggle to hold back a flood of emotion. He didn't blame her. She'd had a tough time on this level and the next wouldn't be any easier. Marcus put his arm around her shoulders and she buried her face in his chest.

He had to admit, it wasn't fair. They had been through so much on this level and now there was nothing to show for it. Nothing. No new weapons; no new magic; no new skills to speak of, except the small amount of knife-throwing practice he'd had. By this time, they were supposed to have gained enough weapons and experience to be able to defeat Zhudai. Instead, they were further behind than ever.

Vishnu's face softened into resigned understanding.

"Hasn't your father always chided you for expecting life to be fair, child? And yet still you do so."

Jade jerked her head up and stared at him, her expression dumbfounded. Phoenix blinked. How could a god of this world possibly know what her real-world father had said to her? How?

Tears sparkled on her cheeks. Before anyone could stop her, she wrenched free of Marcus and ran out of the room. Phoenix yelled her name as she fled but she ignored him. He and Marcus took several hasty steps toward the door. Vishnu called them back.

"Let her go!"

The command in his voice was impossible to disobey. Reluctantly and resentfully, they returned.

"Yajat might still be out there," Phoenix argued. "She's not safe."

"She is following her destiny. She is where she is meant to be. Leave her."

Again Phoenix found it impossible to ignore the god's tone. Seething, he glared at the blue-skinned deity.

"There are things to finish before I must return to my own realm." Vishnu stepped back onto the plinth where his statue had stood. The companions watched him. He nodded regally to them.

"Outside, you will find a gate that will take you to your next quest. Cadoc." He sent a warning look toward the other Player. "You have a chance. Don't throw this one away. Redeem yourself before you move on. You may not find Jupiter and his fellow gods of Rome quite as understanding as I."

Cadoc screwed up his face and nodded, scratching his chin.

"Phoenix." The god turned fathomless eyes his way. "You and your companions will have every skill and every tool you need to succeed. Many of them you simply have not yet recognised for what they are. Now you need to follow through to the end what you have begun. Restore balance to this land and to yourselves. You have just three days until the *ri shi*. If you have not completed your task by then, you are lost and this world and your own will belong to Zhudai."

He eyed each of them until, one by one, they dropped their gazes, unable to meet his knowing, infinitely wise and dark gaze. There was an odd, cracking sound and a half-seen flash of purple-blue non-light that made them blink. When they looked up, the statue was again in place: complete with Sudarshana glinting in its hand. The light disappeared, along with the last of Jade's little lights, leaving them in silent darkness.

"Um..." Brynn's small voice sounded beside Phoenix's elbow. "Do you think we could get out of here now? This is just plain creepy."

"Sounds good to me."

Slowly, they felt and blundered their way out of the dark temple, into the open air of the courtyard. They peered around but Yajat and his men were nowhere to be seen.

Not far away, Jade leaned with her head against the neck of her mare, stroking its nose. She seemed ok. Phoenix hoped he wouldn't have to deal with her right now. He had no idea what you were supposed to say to a girl when she was upset. He looked at Marcus, who frowned and shrugged.

"I think she just needs a little time to rest and regain her real strength." He sent a quick glare at Cadoc; who had the grace to look sheepish. "So what do we do with *him?*" Marcus jerked his chin at the Player.

Phoenix ran his fingers through his hair. "Good question. What do we do with you, Cadoc? You almost cost us the level and you owe Jade at least three lives." Feeling his blood start to boil at the thought of their supposed friends' treachery, he reached for Blódbál.

"Hey, cut me some slack." Cadoc stepped a pace back, raising his own hands to show they were empty. "I didn't know you when Bhumaka and Yajat hired me. As far as I knew, you were just a job. I didn't even know you were Players until the morning *after* we fought the Naga. By then I'd already slipped Jade one dose of poison. With Bhumaka's army expecting us, what was I supposed to do? I figured the best way out for all of us was to at least get out of his camp."

"And why didn't you tell us when we reached Guatamiputra's camp then?" Phoenix demanded, his sword half-raised, its death-songs loud in his head.

"By then we'd met Sopaniputra," Cadoc explained, "and killing him really *was* my Quest. I was supposed to clear the way for Vasi to take the throne after his father. Apparently he'll be a better ruler. I figured you might not approve of that, either, so it seemed safest to shut the heck up and play it by ear."

"And poisoning Jade? The Sudarshana? Vishnu's weapons?"

Cadoc grimaced. "I actually didn't give Jade anything else after that night on the mountain. She just reacted really badly to the herbal sleeping drug Bhumaka gave me. I tried giving her the antidote a few times after we escaped but it seemed to make her worse. I don't know why."

Phoenix exchanged looks with Marcus. The story sounded plausible. They had experience with how susceptible Jade was to certain herbs.

"Why did Bhumaka let us go at all? Why didn't he just kill us there and then in his camp?" Marcus put in.

The Player shrugged. "I thought that *was* the plan but evidently he'd decided that Jade's link to the Manasa devi could be useful. He thought Manasa could control her enough to kill Guatamiputra up close and win the war. I think that was his own idea, though, not Yajat's. It's all a bit political for me, to be honest."

Phoenix closed his eyes. It sounded plausible enough but the Player was good at sounding plausible.

Cadoc continued. "Here in the temple, I knew Yajat was somewhere around. If I'd blown the whistle then, we'd all be dead." He ruefully fingered the bloody tear in his shirt. "I must admit, I wasn't expecting him to kill me so soon. S'pose I really should have, though. And I did save Brynn, after all."

Marcus laid a hand on Phoenix's arm. "Do you remember what Anuket said would happen when we returned the Sudarshana?"

Phoenix shook his head irritably, not quite ready to let go of his annoyance with Cadoc.

"She said this quest would unite a kingdom; someone who had wronged would be redeemed; and that something broken would be fixed," Marcus reminded him.

"Actually," Jade cut in quietly, "she said '*a path will be taken that will make whole what is torn asunder.*'"

The others looked at her. In the faint glow of her witchlights they saw her eyes were swollen from crying. She seemed calm enough now.

"Well," Brynn shook his head, "that's stupidly cryptic. What path? What's been torn asunder? Have we already taken the path and fixed it without knowing? Gods. Honestly. First riddles, now no rewards. I've just about had it with gods. I'm going to find the gate. I told you Cadoc was no good and you ignored me, so now you decide what to do with him." He threw up his hands and stalked away, muttering.

Phoenix was relieved to see Jade smile slightly. "So," he raised an eyebrow at her, "he probably did worse to you than any of us. What do you think we should do with him?"

Jade shrugged. "It doesn't matter. He's only got this life left. Let him try to finish his last level. I don't care."

Cadoc swept her a deep bow, grinning as he caught her

hand up for a flourishing kiss. "You are as kind as you are beautiful, my lady."

"Oh, stop it," she snapped. "I've had enough of you stupid men and your stupid macho egos. Let's just get on with the next quest. I want to go home." Her voice cracked a little on the last word and Phoenix realised she was still emotionally strung out. It was probably best to get Cadoc out of sight as fast as possible.

Brynn's faint *halloo* brought them all to his side. He had found the next gate. The three-stone doorway was set into the stone wall surrounding the temple complex. An ornate painting depicting Jade's ride on Garuda's back was splashed across the walls on either side, just as Vasi had described. They gathered around the gate and Cadoc stepped up with his hand outstretched.

He hesitated. "Before I go, I've got some gifts for you." Rummaging in his saddlebags, he produced a small, rolled up piece of black cloth. Handing it to Brynn, he quirked his characteristic grin. "Brynn, I heard you lost your set and I've got a spare now that Llew's gone."

Brynn unrolled the cloth and gave a little squeak of joy. "Lockpicks! Fantastic!" He changed his expression to a frown again. "I mean…thanks. Maybe I'll think about forgiving you one day. At least you finally remembered my name."

Cadoc laughed and reached out to ruffle the boy's hair. Brynn swatted his hand away irritably. The Player's smile twisted and he turned to Phoenix.

"This is for you. With a little practice, you'll be pretty good." The prince handed him a leather belt. Into it were slotted five throwing knives.

Phoenix shook his head and tried to hand it back. "These are your main weapons."

"Nah. They were Llew's, too. You may as well use them. He was really bad at it anyway. Here Marcus." Cadoc handed the Roman a bundle of arrows. "I saw you were getting low and grabbed a handful from the Raj's fletcher."

Marcus accepted them with a nod and a handshake.

"And last but not least," he gave a small package to Jade, "I picked this up on my Level Three: in Luoyang, the capital of the Han Empire in China."

The companions stared at him in shock. He nodded ruefully.

"That's where I met Yajat, actually. He's Zhudai's pet assassin and when he found out I was coming here next, he took me to Xijing where Zhudai's holed up. They hired me on as an extra hand in case he couldn't find you in time."

"Did you ever meet Zhudai, himself?" Phoenix asked.

"Nah, he was busy interrogating some important prisoner in his dungeon." Cadoc dismissed their arch-enemy with a shrug. "The palace gossip was that he's trying to find a way to become immortal. The Han Emperor was even supposed to be coming out from Luoyang to investigate. I wouldn't take it too seriously, though. Zhudai's got everyone so scared in Xijing that they'd believe anything about him."

Jade finished unwrapping the soft cloth around her gift and let out a sigh of awe. She held the object up, admiring its pale translucency in the moonlight.

"It's beautiful," she breathed. She slipped the ring onto her right hand and turned it. It was a yin-yang symbol.

"The band is green jade," Cadoc said diffidently, "but the symbol is white, imperial jade with a black pearl inlay. When I saw your amulet, I figured you might like it. It's not magic or anything but it's nice."

"I love it," she smiled shyly at him. "My name's actually Jade Pearl, so it's perfect. Thankyou."

Cadoc grabbed his horse's reins and turned back toward the gate. "Anyway. I think I've redeemed myself enough, don't you? I'd better go before things get too sentimental. Good luck with your last level. I don't expect I'll make it through but it's been fun. See you on the outside."

With a jaunty wave and a blown kiss to Jade, he touched the gate and said 'Rome'. The portal shimmered to life. Cadoc stepped through without a backward look.

And was gone.

The companions were silent, staring at the now-empty portal, each lost in their own thoughts. Finally, Phoenix shook himself and glanced at the others.

"Well, I guess it's time we moved on, too."

He reached out a hand to touch the cold stone but never made contact. From out of the darkness swept a swift shadow, knocking his arm aside and shoving him roughly to the ground. He fell awkwardly, landing hard on his right elbow and hip as he turned to try and see what had hit him.

Marcus' deep voice raised in anger and Brynn's lighter one cried Jade's name. Phoenix struggled to his feet, trying to ignore the sharp pain in his arm as he reached for his sword.

Jade shouted something, her voice somehow muffled. There were sounds of a struggle then her white face was illuminated by the glow of the portal. Someone had activated it – someone who also held Jade captive in his arms; his dark hand over her mouth. Phoenix caught a glimpse of what looked like thin iron chain wrapped around her neck and arms. Behind her, he saw the darkly handsome face of Yajat, the assassin. Teeth flashed white in the darkness as their enemy flung Jade bodily through the glistening portal.

Phoenix started forward to follow. The assassin shook his finger warningly and dropped a small pot on the ground. With a laugh, he dived through the gate and vanished. Phoenix stared for half a second at the sputtering, sparking wick poking out of the pot and felt a surge of fear.

"Get back!   Get back!" he yelled at his astonished friends. "Run!" Turning, he sprinted away from the portal, waving his arm to spook the horses.

A thunderous concussion of noise and white-red light slammed into his back, sending him tumbling and flying across the courtyard.

Stunned, Phoenix lay on the cold stone, his head buried under his arms until a small shower of stone dust eased. Sitting gingerly up, he turned back, hoping against hope that the gate had survived the blast.

It had not.

The three-stone portal into the next level was now a tumbled pile of broken rock and a gaping hole in the stone wall. Next to it, lying forlornly on the ground, was Jade's quarterstaff.

Jade was gone and so was the only way to get to her.

EPILOGUE

Phoenix pushed himself to his feet. His right arm hurt but there were more important things to worry about.

"Brynn? Marcus? Are you alright?" he called into the grey-blackness of the night.

His vision was still half-obscured by sparkles of white and red afterimages from the blast.

There were groans off to the right, so he fumbled his way over. Brynn and Marcus helped each other up. They were white with dust but otherwise unhurt.

"What on earth was *that?*" Marcus sounded shellshocked. "Magic?"

"No," Phoenix said grimly, "I think the Chinese have discovered gunpowder."

"Gunpowder?"

"It's an explosive," Phoenix said shortly, holding his right arm across his chest. It hurt badly now.

"I think we figured that out," Marcus said dryly. "Yajat has Jade. He's taken her to Xijing – I heard him when he touched the gate. He…he was too fast for me to stop him. I'm sorry."

Phoenix shook his head. "He was too fast for all of us. I just hope the iron chains mean he wants her alive now, rather than dead. If she's still alive, we have a chance."

"What do you mean, 'a chance'?" Brynn said shrilly. "This gate is destroyed and the other one is in the Naga caves, totally blocked by a rockslide. How are we supposed to get to her? How far away is Xijing?"

"Way too far to get there riding straight." Phoenix shook his head. "But there's a quicker way."

Marcus drew a sharp breath. "The gate Cadoc came through. Where did he say it was?"

"Karla Caves!" Brynn said breathlessly. "Of course. Let's go!"

"Three problems," Phoenix said faintly.

"What?" Marcus and Brynn turned on him together.

"One, we don't know where it is; two the horses bolted; and three," he sat down on a piece of rock, feeling extremely unwell, "I think I've broken my arm."

Marcus swore and knelt in front of him, feeling the arm until Phoenix almost fainted with the pain.

"Brynn, go find the horses. I'll set the bone then we'll ride for the Raj's camp. Vasi will know where these caves are." He caught Phoenix's eye. "We'll find her, Phoenix. I promise. We'll find her and we'll destroy Zhudai. Now take a deep breath. This will hurt."

Phoenix nodded gratefully. Then, as Marcus gripped his arm firmly, he passed into blessed unconsciousness.

*****

Somewhere beneath the Emperor's summer palace in Xijing, his prisoner moaned. Baiyu held his head in his hands and sank to the ground in despair. They had been separated. It was the worst thing that could have happened. Together, Jade and Phoenix might have been able to defeat Zhudai. Apart, they were weakened.

Jade was close. Baiyu could sense her – but so fragile and so withdrawn that he doubted she would survive even one night in Zhudai's cold, lightless dungeons. Baiyu shivered. If she wasn't able to fight the mental and physical weakness that drained her… If she lost her last lives here… Then Zhudai would succeed – and if Zhudai succeeded in becoming an Immortal, both this world and theirs would be changed forever.

High above, in his austere room, Zhudai dismissed Yajat with a rare word of praise. Moments later, the sorcerer's triumphant laughter rang through the palace, causing servants to cower in fear and the young Han Emperor himself to stir uneasily in his sleep.

THE END

*****

Appendix

Naga–many Indian people believe the Naga are a snake-people dwelling underground and protecting treasures. The word Naga comes from the ancient Sanskrit language, and "nag" is still the word for snake in most of the languages of India. They are considered nature spirits and the protectors of springs, wells and rivers. They bring rain, and thus fertility, but are also thought to bring disasters such as floods and drought.

Since Nagas have an affinity with water, the entrances to their underground palaces are often said to be hidden at the bottom of wells, deep lakes and rivers. Varuna, the Vedic god of storms, is viewed as the King of the Nagas. According to some traditions Nagas are only malevolent to humans when they have been mistreated.

Cadoc is Welsh for "battle"

Punya-Vishaya is the modern city of Pune. It was, in ancient times, just a small, agricultural market town. Pune (pronounced: *Poon-eh)*. It is inland of the ancient port of Mumbai/Bombay/Śūrpāraka

Śūrpāraka: (or Soupara) is the ancient Sanskrit name for the port of Bombay (now called Mumbai). It was a large trading port on the western coast of India.

The Sakas: Were the Scythian peoples who originally lived in the eastern part of Central Asia. They are considered to be of north-eastern Iranian people. They lived in what is now Kazakhstan, Uzbekistan, Tajikistan; moving east into parts of Afghanistan, parts of Pakistan, parts of India in the centuries before 300AD.

The **Western Satraps**, or **Western Kshatrapas:** The word *Kshatrapa* stands for *satrap*, which means viceroy or governor of a province. So the Western Kshatrapas were a province of India between 35 and 405AD

Bhumaka: Kshaharata Bhumaka(?-119 AD) was a Western Kshatrapa ruler of the late 1stcentury AD. He was the father of the great Kshatrapa Nahapana, who was later defeated by Guatamiputra Sakartani of the Satavahana Empire.

The **names** Jade chooses for them in India all have meaning in the ancient Sanskrit language spoken there.
Bala (Brynn) = Sanskrit boy name meaning "Child, young one"
Marut (Marcus) = Sanskrit boy name meaning "The Wind"
Chandak (Cadoc) = Sanskrit boy name meaning "the Moon"
Pran (Phoenix) = Sanskrit boy name meaning "Life"
Jaya (Jade) = Sanskrit girl name meaning "victory"

Guatamiputra Satakarni was the most famous king of the Satavahana dynasty. It is believed that he ruled from about 80AD until about 130AD. He defeated the Saka Katrap Nahapana (son of Bhumaka) to regain the western part of his empire. He also defeated armies of the Sakas (Scythians), Yavanas (Greeks) and Pahlavas (Parithans).

His son, **Vasisthiputra** Sri Pulamavi, ruled at Paithan on the banks of Godavari River, from about 130AD.

Putra, in the ancient Sanskrit language, means 'son of a king'.

Castes: Hindu society is traditionally categorized into four classes, called *Varnas*..

1) The lowest of the Varnas was the **Shudras** - the servants and farmhands who did not own their own business or their own land, and who had to work for other people. Probably the largest number of people belonged to this caste.

2) Above them were the **Vaishyas**, or farmers and traders, who owned their own farms or businesses.

3) Above these were the **Kshatriya,** or warriors. There were not very many true Kshatriyas. A lot of them were in the army, or leaders in other ways. Women could not be warriors, but if they were born into a Kshatriya family, they were still of that caste and could only marry into that caste.

4) The most powerful caste was the **Brahmins,** the priests and leaders. There were only a few of them. Only Brahmin men were allowed to go to school, or to teach in schools (Brahmin women could not go to school).

Guatamiputra and his family are believed to have been from this caste.

People who came from different castes could not eat together. Usually people from one caste did not marry or make friends with people from another caste.

Below the four Varnas, were the **Untouchables** of no caste. Below the Untouchables were the **slaves**. Untouchables usually did the worst jobs, like cleaning up people's poop from the gutters, or collecting garbage

Vishnu is one of the many aspects of the Supreme God, Brahman, according to the Hindu belief system. Hinduism is a very complex, very diverse set of beliefs. Common themes include:

A) **Devas** (hundreds of gods who are just various aspects of Brahman) coming to earth as *avatars*

B) **Dharma**–ethics, morals & duties;

C) **Samsara**– the continuing cycle of birth, life, death and rebirth (reincarnation)

D) **Karma**– action and consequence/reaction;

E) **Moksha**– the freedom from *Samsara*

F) **Yoga**– various forms of paths, practices and meditations.

There are many fascinating tales, poems and stories from thousands of years of Hindu beliefs in the gods. Most Hindus favour one or more aspects of Brahman and pay respects to the god that represents that best. For example: Shiva represents destruction or transformation; Ganeshi is the remover of obstacles.

The **urumi or chuttuval** is a long sword made of flexible steel, sharp enough to cut into flesh, but flexible enough to be rolled into a tight coil. It was used and still can be found in Kerala, India and is one of the weapons learned by practitioners of the martial art of Kalaripayattu.

Onager: The Roman catapult, the onager, (Latin for wild ass because it had a kick like a donkey when the arm was released), was a very large and cumbersome piece of equipment. It could fire rocks of up to 150 lbs (70 kgs) to be used to smash through walls and fortifications. It could also be loaded with the equivalent mass of smaller stones or fiery pitch to use against enemy troops or to bombard the inside of a fort.

Garuda. In Hindu mythology, Garuda is usually the mount (vahanam) of Vishnu. Garuda is often depicted as being an eagle or a half-eagle: having a golden body, white face, red wings, and an eagle's head, but with a man's body. Legend says he will only acknowledge a true king. He has been a long-time enemy of the Naga.

Pataleshwar Cave Temple: dedicated to Lord Pataleshwar - God of the Underworld, dates back to the eighth century. One of the major attractions of the Pataleshwar Cave Temple of Pune is its exquisite rock-cut architecture. The cave temple also comprises of a shrine, dedicated to Lord Shiva. The rocks of the cave, cut into pillars, seating areas and akin rooms, are as old as 700-800 AD, so it's later than in this story. The Shiva shirne is situated in a cube-shaped room, located in the middle of the Temple. Adorned with ornate carvings, the temple also houses the idols of Lord Rama, Sita, Laxmana, Lord Ganesh and Goddess Lakshmi.

A Taste of things to come:

80AD Book Five.

The Yu Dragon

CHAPTER ONE

Phoenix gritted his teeth, wishing his horse came with shock absorbers. Every jarring hoof-beat lanced pain through his arm. Marcus had set the bone well enough but he really needed Jade's healing powers. How was he supposed to swing a sword now?

Pushing the thought aside, he stretched out one leg, easing a bruised butt cheek off the saddle. It didn't help much. They had ridden non-stop since before dawn in an effort to reach Karla Caves. It was taking longer than he'd expected to make their way west. The road toward the coast seethed with refugees from the recently-ended war between the Kshatrapa Bhumaka and the true king, Guatamiputra Sakatarni. Their pathetic footslogging pace made for slow going on the narrow path through the mountains.

Several times, Phoenix had to physically bite his lip to stop himself from shouting at the peasant-soldiers trudging homeward. He just didn't have the patience to deal with this right now. They had to get to Karla Caves and the portal gate to China quickly, or any hope of rescuing Jade would be gone.

For all he knew, she could have already lost her three

remaining lives and be dead. A spasm of fear twisted his guts. His mind shied away from the thought but Phoenix forced himself to consider the possibility. If Jade had lost all her lives and was really dead then he was stuck here. Forever.

He glanced around at the dramatic, tropical, humid landscape. A rugged mountain range rose before him, signalling an abrupt end to the enormous Deccan Plateau at his back. So different from the soft, cool greens of England. The heat of the sun; the dark greens of the forest; the heavy, cloying scents of the jungle; even the food wasn't like Indian food at home in the twenty-first century.

It seemed a long time since he'd seen his mother, his home, his own time. Memories of his old life were fading: being a thirteen year old at school, aikido training, playing computer games and even the harsh reality of his fathers' death and his stepfather's stupidity were all more like a dream. Reality was here in 80AD, India: wars, gods, magic, friends and foes. It wasn't even that great a reality any more. What had been a brilliant adventure to start with now, frankly, sucked.

He'd just about had enough.

A wave of despair swept through him and he had to swallow hard to keep down a groan. He had come to rely on Jade in the last few weeks. She'd been gone just one day and he felt her absence keenly. Everything seemed harder without her quick wits, magical abilities and commonsense. He even missed her pointless worrying. They'd been unwillingly and unwittingly thrown together in this surreal game-world over three weeks ago. During their first few days here Phoenix had, in his carefree impatience to be adventuring, wished her away a dozen times or more. In the past day, since her kidnapping, he'd begged every god he knew, and he'd met several now, to bring her back.

It hadn't worked.

After a full-scale war the day before and hardly any sleep since her abduction, Phoenix now ran on faint hope and sheer determination. He looked across at his grim-faced companions and realised they must be just as weary; just as worried.

Marcus, the battle-hardened son of a Roman Governor, looked older than his sixteen years. His dark, curling hair stuck to his forehead as the sun baked them all in its tropical heat. With soldier's train alertness, his dark eyes swept the surrounds constantly, seeking danger.

Glancing to his left, Phoenix saw Vasi, son of Guatamiputra, riding easily beside Brynn, the youngest of their group. Vasi was clearly tired but Brynn looked worse. The ten year old boy-thief from ancient Britain winced with every hoofbeat. His usually-cheerful, thin was face screwed into a bizarre cross between determination and pain. The pony tossed its head and Brynn's eyes widened in alarm. He wasn't a very good rider.

Prince Vasi, a native of the area, looked the most comfortable in the afternoon heat. His brown skin barely glowed with sweat and he still moved effortlessly in the saddle.

It was due to his father's generosity and gratitude that they were on the road so quickly this morning. Vasi knew the way to Karla Caves and his father provided fresh horses and supplies. Even if they kept going at this slow pace, they should be at the caves before dark.

That hope was dashed the very next moment. Vasi threw up a hand and pulled his mount to a halt. Behind, a servant, leading six spare horses, followed suit. Phoenix frowned and dragged back on the reins. Vasi swung down from his horse, leading it off the track, into the shade of an enormous fig tree. His servant followed.

"What are you doing?" Phoenix demanded. "We don't have time for this. We're already a night and most of a day behind Jade. If we don't reach the Caves soon, we may as well have climbed over the Himalayas into China to get to her."   He flung his good hand at the distant, purple mountains to the northeast.

Vasi calmly sank into a cross-legged position on the ground and nodded to his man.

"We need to eat and the horses need to rest. There's a stream over there. We'll water them and move on when we are all recovered."

Phoenix slipped awkwardly off his horse, holding his broken right arm out so it wouldn't be knocked. His foot caught in the stirrup and he had to hop a few times before it came loose. Brynn snickered, hiding his mouth with his hand. Phoenix glared at him.

"You think this is funny?" He heard the angry edge to his own voice and snapped his jaw shut.

Brynn sobered, staring back at him with solemn, dark eyes.

"Sorry," Phoenix muttered, turning away.

Out of habit, his left hand rested on the hilt of his sword, Blódbál. Its berserker song of glory and death swelled in his head, trying to take over his thoughts and emotions; trying to turn him into the ultimate, amoral warrior. He snatched his hand away, shaken by the power of the song. His emotions were all over the place and the enchanted sword was trying to seize the opportunity to use him as a weapon against his enemies. He had to be careful. If he let it take over he would turn berserker – no longer able to tell enemies from friends.

Right at the moment, though, he would welcome a few enemies to go berserk on. Inaction was driving him nuts.

Sitting down with a thump, Phoenix dropped his head into his good hand and scrubbed fingers through sweaty hair. His right arm throbbed, the fingers fat and stiff. Sharp shafts of pain shot up into his shoulder, dragging at his resolve and strength. Sighing, he closed his eyes. Despair tightened like a band around his chest again. He pressed his lips together.

This couldn't be happening. It just couldn't. Jade couldn't have lost all her lives and have left him here alone. Surely, when he opened his eyes, she would be sitting right across from him, looking anxious, ready to fix his arm and tell him exactly what he'd done wrong so he could argue with her.

Half-hopeful, Phoenix opened his eyes. There, sitting across from him looking faintly concerned, was not her fair, green-eyed, Elven face but Marcus' handsome, square-jawed one.

"Gaaah!" Anger burst free and flooded his belly with fire.

Phoenix sprang up. Marcus stood as well, laying a hand on his own sword, his expression watchful. His friend's caution inflamed Phoenix's mood further. He glared at the Roman, grabbed awkwardly at Blódbál and wrestled the magic sword from its sheath with his left hand.

"Get out of my way, Marcus," he warned.

Sitting around was pointless. If Jade was stupid enough to get herself captured and Vasi wasn't going to help then he would have to go find her, himself.

Marcus eyed him, circling to stay between him and the horses. "What are you going to do?"

"Go get that stupid girl on my own, since you lot are too pathetic to do it with me," Phoenix growled.

Blódbál's music rose and fell in his head; a symphony eagerly urging him on, feeding his anger at Jade and turning it toward Marcus as the nearer target.

"You can't save her on your own," Marcus reasoned. "You're injured and exhausted. You wouldn't be able to fight anyone at the moment and you know it."

His logic annoyed Phoenix further. Marcus was *always* calm. Faced with death and danger, he barely even blinked an eye. It was irritating. In fact, he decided, it was about time someone taught the arrogant Roman a thing or two.

"Y'think, do you?" he sneered. "I can beat you any day."

Marcus slid his sword free, his eyes following Phoenix's slightest movement. "Maybe, right-handed but left-handed? I doubt it." His derisive chuckle inflamed Phoenix's rage until it consumed his thoughts.

"Marcus?" Brynn's question was loaded with doubt.

"Shut up," the Roman gestured the boy back, "I know what I'm doing."

"Somehow, I doubt that," Phoenix mocked. "You're always letting Jade do the thinking for you. What are you going to do now she's not here? No-one to worship and slobber over now. She's *gone*. She's left us to fend for ourselves. She's probably dead by now and I'm *stuck* here with you. That's what people do. They leave when you need them. So why don't you go, too, Marcus? I know you only came with us because of *her*," Phoenix taunted, his mind filled with fury - anger at Jade for being stupid; anger at Marcus for turning against him. He would leave too, so what was the point in prolonging it? He wasn't needed anyway. Phoenix didn't need anyone.

He lunged, stabbing with the tip of his sword. Marcus twisted aside but Phoenix had seen the flash of real fear in the Roman's eyes and he exulted at it. Blódbál urged him on, flooding his mind with the desire to give in to the blood-rage. If he did, Blódbál promised, he would never be unhappy again; never be frightened; never be alone.

Finally, tired of fighting it; tired of being scared and alone, Phoenix did what he had sworn to Thor and his friends he would not. He let go. Letting down his mental barriers against the sword, he felt its full power pour into his soul and rejoiced in the molten, mad energy it gave him.

Now, his enemies would see his *real* power. The time had come to kill them all. Starting with this cocky little Roman in front of him.

*****

THE END

Discover other titles by Aiki Flinthart at:
http://aikiflinthart.weebly.com/

The 80AD series
(YA Adventure/Fantasy)

80AD Book 1: *The Jewel of Asgard*
80AD Book 2: *The Hammer of Thor*
80AD Book 3: *The Tekhen of Anuket*
80AD Book 4: *The Sudarshana*
80AD Book 5: *The Yu Dragon*

The Kalima Chronicles
(YA Adventure/Fantasy)

IRON (Book 1)

ABOUT THE AUTHOR

Aiki Flinthart lives in Australia. In between running a business and being with her husband of many years, she pursues writing, archery, knife-throwing, martial arts, art, music, bellydancing and watches too much television. After many years of writing for her own amusement, she finally decided to write for others' – and discovered it was even more fun.

Discover other titles by Aiki Flinthart at:
http://aikiflinthart.weebly.com/

Connect with Aiki on Facebook